ラフカディオ・ハーンの英語教育
Lafcadio Hearn's English Lessons

《友枝高彦・高田力・中土義敬のノートから》

【監修】
富山大学附属図書館ヘルン文庫
平川祐弘

弦書房

目　次

英文序文（English Foreword）……………………………………………………4

まえがき ……………………………………………………………………………7

講義ノート『熊本高校時代に於ける Lafcadio Hearn の英語教授』
筆写原版・復元・日本語訳 ……………………………………………………21

Country　国、田舎　　27

Fune　船　　29

Ike　池　　29

Colors　色　　31

Trees, Plants, Vegetables, Grass & c.　木、植物、野菜、草など　　35

Sounds　音　　41

Takai　高い　　45

Hone to Kawa　骨と皮　　49

Climate and Weather　気候と天候　　51

Wind　風　　51

Birds　鳥　　55

About parts of the body　体の部位について　　57

City, Town, Village, Hamlet　都会、町、村、村落　　63

Time　時間　　67

Prepositions of Time　時の前置詞　　69

Earthquakes!　地震だ！　　73

The Sky　空　　81

Preliminary Exercises on prepositions　前置詞の予備練習　　85

Prepositions of Places　場所の前置詞　　91

If with Tenses　If と時制　　95

Rules of Shall and Will　Shall と Will のルール　　97

Rules for exclamatory phrases　感嘆文のルール　　101

Rules for questions or interrogative phrases　疑問文のルール　　103

Exercises on the Articles　冠詞の練習　　111

Examples of this Modification or Particularization 　修飾または特定化の例　　113
Exceptions to General Rules of the Article "the" 　定冠詞 the の一般的ルールの例外　　117
About verbs used wrongly by students 　学生が間違って使う動詞について　　121

『熊本高校時代に於ける Lafcadio Hearn の英語教授』
　の内容とその意義 ……………………………………………………………127

出版にあたって……………………………………………………………………141

あとがき……………………………………………………………………………143

English Foreword

This is the reproduction of a notebook of English lessons given by Lafcadio Hearn(1850-1904) as taken down word for word by one of his Kumamoto high school students, Tomoeda Takahiko (1876-1957). Tomoeda learnt English from Hearn from autumn 1893-spring 1894. It was Hearn's third and last year at Kumamoto Daigo Kōtō-Chūgakkō. As Alan Rosen remarks in his English foreword to *Lafcadio Hearn's Student Composition Corrections,* a preceding book published by the same Gen Shobo Company in 2011, the writer Hearn was by all accounts a most conscientious and inspiring teacher of English. This is true not only as a middle school teacher in his Matsue days (September 1890-November 1891) but also as a high school teacher in his Kumamoto period (November 1891-July 1894) and, we may add, as a university lecturer in his Tokyo years (September 1896-September 1904).

How the Tomoeda notebook, or more precisely its copy of a copy, was found by Senda Atsushi and Mari Christine is a very interesting story. In the mid-1940s Tomoeda, retired professor of ethics, at Tokyo Bunrika Daigaku (present-day Tsukuba University), visited his former student Takata Tsutomu (1893-1946) who was then a teacher at Toyama High School. Takata, editor of *Japanese Stories from Lafcadio Hearn* (London: Kegan Paul, 1933), was a Hearn scholar who had compiled the catalogue of the Lafcadio Hearn Library in the Toyama High School in 1927. When Takata invited the old professor to see the Hearn Library, Tomoeda told Takata that he had kept a notebook of Lafcadio Hearn's English lessons taken down almost half a century before.

Takata borrowed the notebook from his former professor. Reading through Tomoeda's notebook, he was amazed at the high quality of Hearn's lessons, and tried to publish the notebook in book form. Takata contacted Nakatsuchi Yoshitaka of the Hokuseido Press Tokyo, a Toyama man, and Nakatsuchi too found the notebook to be a remarkably good English teaching material for Japanese students. The Hokuseido Press, having published many of Lafcadio Hearn's writings both in English and in Japanese translation, was a very creditable company with an excellent publishing record. This is clear if one looks at Perkins's *Bibliography of Lafcadio Hearn.* Nakatsuchi discreetly took good care of Hearn's heritage. Together with Nannichi Tsunetaro, his uncle and the Director of the Toyama High School, Tanabe Ryuji, Nannichi's brother and a former student of Hearn, and Nakatsuchi had successfully negotiated with the Koizumi family for the purchase of the 2435 books in possession of the late Lafcadio Hearn, also known as Koizumi Yakumo. In this way the Hearn Library was presented to the Toyama High School in celebration of the opening of the institution in 1924 thanks to Madame Baba Haruko's magnificent donation. The House of Baba was and still is a prominent family in Toyama.

The war against English speaking countries broke out in 1941. The Hokuseido Press, however, continued the publication of English books. For example, it published in 1942 R. H. Blyth's *Zen in English Literature and Oriental Classics,* although the author himself was interned in a camp near Kobe as a British subject. However, as for *Lafcadio Hearn's English Lessons,* the publication was not possible. The war situation began to deteriorate in the Southern Pacific, and the Hokuseido Press could not get permission from Nippon Shuppan-kai (wartime semi-governmental organization in charge of the distribution of publishing material) for the publication of the book in September 1943. Nakatsuchi, however, as a very resourceful man, believed that it might be published one day, and he recopied meticulously with his pen the forty-odd pages of Tomoeda's notebook previously copied and prepared for publication by Takata before returning it to its owner. Tomoeda's original notebook must have been burned together with Tomoeda's Tokyo house by the indiscriminate American air raid in April 1945. Takata survived the bombardment in Toyama but died in January 1946, and his copy too seemed to have been lost. As the publisher Nakatsuchi himself died in February 1945 before the end of the Pacific War, no one thought any more of the publication of Tomoeda's notebook. It was completely forgotten.

This is how Nakatsuchi's copy of Tomoeda's notebook was recently found. Senda Atsushi is a Toyama businessman, relative of the Nakatsuchi family. Senda once lived in Nakatsuchi's Tokyo house in his student days in the 1960s. When a new family took over the Hokuseido Press, Senda received all the documental materials of the former owners, Nakatsuchi and his son. In case they contained valuable publishing records or other objects concerning Lafcadio Hearn, Senda checked them before donating them all to Toyama University, and he incidentally found the notebook in question. When Mari Christine, a media personality and an associate of Senda, was invited by Toyama University to promote relations with the general public, Senda showed her the notebook. Here is what she writes: "I was spellbound by its simplicity and beautiful English text. It was difficult to imagine that this was the spoken English of the 1890s. The quality of English words Hearn uses is eternal. Even today, one could use the words and sentences. It is a great English textbook."

She then showed me Tomoeda's notebook when I came to Toyama to give a series of public lectures on Lafcadio Hearn. I immediately recognized its value for Hearn studies apart from its value as an English textbook. Upon my suggestion, Mari Christine and Senda Atsushi went to Buzen City, Tomoeda Takahiko's home town, and met one of Tomoeda's relatives. Among some findings are a picture of Tomoeda taken when he entered Tokyo Imperial University in 1898 and his report card sent by the Fifth High School to his father: Tomoeda was second in his class ranking. By the way we may also note the fact that Tomoeda accompanied Baron Suematsu to London as his secretary during the delicate period of the Russo-Japanese War for the promotion of Anglo-

Japanese friendship.

As for the qualities of Tomoeda's notebook as an English language textbook for Japanese students, I advise serious students to read Professor Nishikawa Morio's introductory essay written in Japanese. From this notebook one can learn not only English but also about Lafcadio Hearn's sense as a writer and teacher. We may also add a final remark by Mari Christine: Hearn's method of teaching reminds us of the way Hearn eventually teaches English to his son Kazuo. It appears in the 1957 book *Re-echo* by Kazuo Koizumi, edited by Nancy Fellers.

I have checked the transcriptions of English phrases and corresponding Japanese translations made by Mari Christine. The Japanese translations have been added so as to make the material more accessible to Japanese who may wish to learn English, using this notebook. Professor Nishikawa of Kumamoto University, who wrote an introductory note to *Lafcadio Hearn's Student Composition Corrections,* has again provided an introductory essay on the significance of *Lafcadio Hearn's English Lessons.* I have written in my Japanese foreword biographical facts about Tomoeda Takahiko, Takata Tsutomu and Nakatsuchi Yoshitaka, and also about Lafcadio Hearn as a teacher. The impression I got from this editing of Tomoeda's notebook is that no real and serious inter-cultural communication, in the days of Lafcadio Hearn as well as in present days, is possible without solid knowledge and deep cultural background.

For their generous financial help we thank Toyama University and especially Mrs Matsui Kumi, granddaughter of Director Nannichi, who eighty-nine years ago founded Toyama High School, the present-day Toyama University.

As for the editors of *Lafcadio Hearn's English Lessons,* we would like to print on the front page the names of the original contributors and actual editors: Tomoeda Takahiko, Takata Tsutomu and Nakatsuchi Yoshitaka.

December 15, 2012, the day of a symposium held at Toyama University on Hearn's interpretation of "Creole Japan."

Sukehiro Hirakawa, Professor Emeritus, Tokyo University

まえがき

平川祐弘

　ラフカディオ・ハーン (Lafcadio Hearn 日本名小泉八雲、1850年6月27日生－1904年9月26日没) の貴重な資料が出てきた。熊本の五高生が筆記したハーンの英語教育の実態を示す筆記ノートの写しが見つかったのである。

　ノートをきちんと取った生徒は友枝高彦といい、明治9年(1876年)11月4日生－昭和32年(1957年)7月7日没である。友枝は豊前大村(現在の福岡県豊前市)の大庄屋の出身で、大村小学校、豊津中学校を経て、熊本の坪井の菓子屋の二階にあったという予備校有進校で2ヵ月英語も習い、明治24年(1891年)9月、熊本の第五高等中学校補充科2級に入学した。満14歳10ヵ月である。当時の校長は友枝が入学したと同じ明治24年に31歳の若さで着任した嘉納治五郎であった。なおハーンは嘉納に遅れて同年11月19日に熊本に到着、駅頭で嘉納校長の出迎えを受けた。嘉納校長は明治26年2月、ハーンは明治27年10月4日に熊本を離れた。友枝は嘉納やとくに秋月悌次郎から強い感化を受けたと『龍南懐古拾遺』(大正15年筆)で述べている。なお夏目漱石は明治29年、1896年春に(当時は改組されて第五高等学校となった)同校に着任したが、友枝は習わなかったようである。

　友枝高彦は熊本第五高等中学校では補充科2級、補充科1級、予科3級、予科2級、予科1級、本科2級、本科1級と計7年を学んだらしい。明治31年(1898年)に卒業した。ハーンから英語を習っていた明治27年の1月から3月にかけての第2学期の予科3級乙の席次は35人のクラスで2番である。当時は席次は父兄に通知されていた。明治31年、東京帝国大学文科大学入学、哲学・倫理学を学んだ。友枝の上京よりも2年早い時期から、正確には明治29年秋からハーンは同じ東大文学部で教えていたから、友枝は大学でもハーンの授業をあるいは受けたかもしれないが、わからない。友枝は明治34年に帝国大学を卒業、大学院に進んだ。その後、友枝は日露開戦に際し政府より英国に派遣された末松謙澄 (1855－1920) の2人の秘書の1人として北米経由で渡英、2年間イギリスに滞在した。末松謙澄はかねて1878年から86年にかけて英国に留学したことのある俊秀で、留学中に『源氏物語』の英訳にとりかかり初めの17章をロンドンで出版にこぎつけた人である。伊藤博文の女婿で、日露戦争に際し英国世論を親日の方向へ動かすために派遣された要員であったから、その秘書もまた英語力が求められたことであったろう。いま1人の秘書は1866年生れの高楠順次郎で、すでに在欧体験7年、著名な仏教学者として知られる。高楠は末松が第3次伊藤内閣で逓信大臣であったときにも秘書官をつとめ、日露戦争勃発時には東大で梵語学を講じていた。末松も友枝もともに豊前出身という同郷の誼もあって連

れて行かれたということも考えられよう。ハーンから英語を習ったとはいえ、そのような大先輩や先輩の下での初めての在外勤務は友枝にとっては相当辛かったに相違ない。庶務的な仕事をしていたのではあるまいか。なお日露戦争中、ひそかに満洲に潜入し、松花江の鉄橋を爆破しようとしてロシア兵に捕えられハルビン郊外で銃殺された沖禎介は友枝の補充2級の同級生であった。目隠しを拒んで泰然として死に就くさまがロンドンの絵入雑誌の戦争口絵に出、友枝はそれを沖君の厳父に呈したこともあった。

　帰国した友枝は熊本の母校で一年教えた後、明治41年京都帝国大学文科大学助教授、明治43年から米国のシカゴ、英国、独逸のベルリン、ライプチッヒなどへ3年間にわたり留学し、ドイツ哲学の教えを受けた。大正9年東京高等師範学校教授となり、昭和4年東京文理科大学が創立されるに及んでその教授となり昭和16年停年退職した。昭和になってからも2度にわたり渡欧、親独派教授として日独友好などにつとめたようである。著書に『師範修身』『中学修身』『女子修身』などがある。豊前市大村に鉄筋平屋建8畳足らずの倉庫が友枝資料館となっているが、あまり利用されていないようである。

　この友枝高彦は明治26年の秋から27年春にかけて第五高等中学校の予科3級の時、ハーンから英語を習い、授業内容を克明にノートした。満16歳から17歳にかけての友枝生徒が習った頃のハーンは満43歳、3年間の熊本生活の最後の年であった。なおハーンはこのノートにかなり近い性質の"Telling the Time by the Clock in English"などの英語教育資料を東京で刊行されていた英語教育雑誌 *The Museum*——一高生だった漱石や子規がマードック先生の授業の際に提出した英文レポートなども載せた月刊誌である——のNo. XIX pages 283-285 にも掲載したことがある。しかし友枝ノートのようにハーンが黒板に書いて声を立てて教えた英語の授業をまざまざと身近に感じさせる生徒側の資料はほかにない。

　その友枝ノートを昭和18年、北星堂が出版する予定で写したもののコピーが富山大学内で見つかったのである。このノートを世に出すことを企てて友枝の筆記帳を写した人は当時の富山高校教授の高田力 (1893 - 1946) である。高田はベーシック英語による *Japanese Stories from Lafcadio Hearn* (London: Kegan Paul, 1933) や『小泉八雲乃横顔』を昭和9年に北星堂から出した初期のハーン研究者でヘルン文庫の整理に尽力した人である。その高田の手になる友枝ノートのコピーをさらにコピーした人は北星堂書店の創業者中土義敬 (1889 - 1945) で、中土はハーンの英文著書を次々と世に出した尊敬すべき出版人であった。この中土による筆記ノートの写しはマリ・クリスティーヌ富山大学客員特別研究員の手で英語はトランスクリプトが試みられ、英語例文には日本語訳文も加えられた。ただし、本書掲載にあたっては、監修者として平川が校閲し、英語のトランスクリプションも日本語訳文も英語教科書として遺漏なきようつとめた。その際、足立杏子氏の助力を得た。こうして『ラフカディオ・ハーンの英語教育』は日の目を見るにいたった次第である。

　発見の詳しい経緯にふれるに先立ち、ハーンその人とこの英語教育資料がもつ意味につ

いて私見を述べたい。小泉八雲の日本名で知られるラフカディオ・ハーンは英国進駐軍軍医の父チャールズ・ブッシュ・ハーンとギリシャ人の母ローザ・カシマティとの間にイオニア海のレフカダ島で生まれた。幼時にダブリンに移り住んだが、戦争花嫁のローザはアイルランドの婚家の生活に馴染めず、夫が旧恋の女性とその連れ子たちと一緒になるに及んで家庭は崩壊した。その際ハーンを引取って育ててくれた裕福な大叔母がハーンが16歳のとき破産するに及んで、少年は寄宿学校の中退を余儀なくされ、文無しで社会のどん底へ突き落とされた。そんなハーンは英国でも米国でも大学へ行っていない。実は高校さえもきちんと出ていない。だが移民先のアメリカ社会で底辺から這い上がって新聞記者となったこの独学の人は、文学者としても教師としても意想外に大した人物であって、幕末の開国以来今日までの150年、ハーンを凌駕する文系の外人教師は来日していないようにさえ思われる。そんなハーンであるからわが国では文学者としてはもとより英語教師としても尊重され尊敬されている。この日本における根強い小泉八雲への高評価と太平洋戦争以来の米英両国におけるハーンへの低評価とは奇妙なコントラストをなしているが、その両者のギャップそのものがいまや比較研究の好主題となり論争の種となっている。こうした明暗を分かつ見方の差とも関係して、英語作家であるにもかかわらず、ハーンについての研究は、彼を嫌い無視しようとする米英よりも彼を愛し尊重しようとする日本の方でむしろ進むこととなった。

　なぜこんな対照的な違いが生じたのか。日本が対米英戦に突入した時、かつて日本に帰化したハーンが——死んだのはすでに40年近い昔だったが——米英人によって憎まれた心理はわからないではない。また一部の西洋人と、それに同調する脳内白人化した日本知識人によって、日本人が小泉八雲を愛するのは彼が美化した明治日本を愛するからだ、と決め付けられた心理もわからないではない。ハーンを愛する人は精神的ヘルニアを病む人だと小馬鹿にする風潮は今日にいたるまで続いている。もっとも日本人の自己陶酔的なナルシシズムないしはナショナリズムがわが国におけるハーン人気の根底にあるのは確かで、その証拠に日本人のハーン礼讃者の多くは来日以前のハーンの作品にはあまり関心を示さない。というかハーン礼讃者の中でハーンの作品を英語できちんと読み、研究書にまで目を通している人はけっして多くはないというのが真相であろう。

　しかしそうはいっても小泉八雲名作選集は確実に読まれている。人間いかに愚かであろうとも、自己愛だけで文学作品をいつまでも愛読するはずもない。『怪談』などの文学作品、『知られぬ日本の面影』などのさとい民俗学的観察をちりばめた紀行文、また『停車場にて』など庶民の気持をとらえた『心』などの日本人論には、ある心の真実が感じられる。それだからこそ日本人は読み続けるのではあるまいか。

　そのハーンは文学者としてだけでなく英語教師としても秀でた。というか良い教師であったからこそ日本人の心の襞（ひだ）もきちんと読める日本解釈者となり得たのであろう。明治23年からの1年間、松江中学校での生活はハーンの『英語教師の日記から』に活写され

ている。ハーンは生徒の英文を丁寧に添削した。2011年アラン・ローゼン・西川盛雄両教授が『ラフカディオ・ハーンの英作文教育』（福岡、弦書房）で2人の生徒大谷正信と田辺勝太郎のノートを復元刊行したところ、同書はハーン関係者やとくに英語教育関係者の目を惹いた。教師ハーンは批評も懇切で行き届いているが、中学生にGhosts(幽霊)とか、What is the most awful thing?(世に最も怖いものは何か？)とか、Why should we venerate our Ancestors?(祖先を敬うべき理由は何か？)とか、Emperor(天皇)とかいう題で英作文を書かせた。それはそんな作文からも日本の子供たちの考え方を知ろうとハーンはつとめていたからである。

　ハーンは明治24年からは3年間、熊本第五高等中学校で教えた（ちなみに同校は明治20年に開学、当初は補充科2年、予科3年、本科2年であったらしい。明治27年に第五高等学校となり、昭和24年に熊本大学となった）。ハーンは明治29年からは6年半、東京帝国大学で英文学を講義し、非常な好評を博した。そのためハーンの後釜に坐った人は、日本人であれ英国人であれ、なにかと前任者と比較されて苦しんだ。留学帰りの新任講師夏目金之助がその苦衷を妻に洩らしたことは夏目鏡子の『思ひ出の記』に出ている。実はそれもあって漱石は東大を辞めたのである。この一事をもってしてもハーンがただ者でなかったことはわかるだろう。ハーンの東大時代の講義録は死後10年、学生の英文ノートを基に復元され『文学の解釈』1部・2部、『詩の鑑賞』、『人生と文学』の4冊がまず米国で刊行されて評判を呼んだ。ついで日本で北星堂から次々と刊行された。ハーンの英文著作は日本のみか中国でも歓迎された。ハーンは東洋人の学生のことも念頭において日本や中国の事情にも言及しつつ英米文学を講義した懇切丁寧な人だったからである。

　このように鳥瞰すると、ハーンの価値は日本では認められ、ハーンの研究は着実に進んでいるような印象を与えるかもしれない。しかしわが国の外国文学研究の通弊は、数は多いが実質に乏しいことで、たとえば熊本はハーン研究が一見盛んな土地のようだが、肝心の熊本時代の「ラフカディオ・ハーンの英語教育」の実態は解明されてこなかった。それどころか英語教師ハーンについての従来の研究で欠落している唯一の時期は五高時代であるとさえ言われてきた[1]。

　しかしそんなことを言い立てても、ハーンが熊本を去ってすでに118年が経っている。そうなってしまえば、ハーンがかつてどのように英語を教えたか、ハーンの授業に連なった人はすべて亡くなった以上、もはや調べるすべもない。そもそもハーンから習った五高出身者が存命中に聞き取り調査をきちんと行なわなかった以上、いまさらシンポジウムを開いてみても新しいことが出て来る道理もない。そんな様であってみれば、有形の資料はもう何も残っていないだろうと思われていたのである。ところがそれがはからずも富山大

1　「熊本第五高等中学校における英会話授業」については東京大学文学部市河文庫収蔵のある学生の筆記ノートが保存されており、それは『ヘルン』29(1992)、30(1993)、31(1994)、32(1995)、34(1997)の5回にわたり故銭本健二島根大学教授の手で翻刻されている。ただしそれは友枝ノートほどきちんと体系的に述べられていない。

学で見つかった。ハーン自身は富山を訪ねたことはない。作品中にも富山への言及はない。それなのにその地で新資料というか旧資料が日の目を見た経緯はこうである。

　富山大学の前身は旧制富山高等学校で、大正12年に創設された。開学に際し初代校長に招かれた富山生れの英学者南日恒太郎は、弟の田部隆次がかつてハーンの学生であった関係から隆次に小泉家に交渉させ、ハーンの旧蔵書を15,000円で買い上げた。それは土地の名家馬場家が資金提供を申し出たお蔭で、富山に7年制高校ができ、ヘルン文庫も富山にある所以である。こうしてハーンの旧蔵書 2,435 冊は現在は富山大学附属図書館の特別の1室に架蔵されている。その管理は一時期ハーンのことはよく知らない天下りの文科省のお役人に任されたこともあったようだが、今ではきちんとした資格ある人が管理に当っており、ハーン関係研究書の収集も引き続き行なわれている。

　明治26年生れの高田力は、北海道師範、東京高等師範を経て東大英文科を大正14年卒業、富山高校に教授として着任、ヘルン文庫所蔵目録を作製した。『小泉八雲乃横顔』に収められた「蔵書より観たる八雲」ではハーンの「多様な蔵書を11項に分類し、各冊数を示す中で教室で語ったハーンの言葉や書物の損傷程度、古本屋のゴム印にまで触れて、その読書傾向、性向、趣味を語り、「蔵書の余白に記入されたる短評」では、オリファントの *The Victorian Age of English Literature*(1892) の 89 ヵ所の書入れを、その対象原文の要約と対比するが、明快な要約のために Quite false! などという評語を通じて客観的な論文でありながらハーンの反応まで捉えている」（平川編『小泉八雲事典』の布村弘執筆の項目「高田力」）。高田力はそのようなハーンを尊敬することの深い英語教授であった。その高田が東京高等師範時代に学んだ友枝高彦教授は、昭和10年代の半ば、すでに教職を退き東京文理科大学名誉教授となっていたが、富山に来た。そのおり高田は旧師をヘルン文庫に案内した。すると友枝が50年前、ハーンの授業に出てその筆記帳をまだ保存していると洩らしたのである。高田は特に懇願してその筆記帳を拝借したが、それを読んだときの感激をその跋にこう綴っている。「私は歓喜と好奇の心で胸をふくらましつゝ、1頁1頁と此の50年前の文字を判読して行くうちに、八雲が極めて忠実懇篤なる良教師であって、教授を初学者に徹底させるために深甚なる工夫を凝らしてゐた事実を知つて今更の如く驚いたのである。」

　高田は友枝に願い出、賛同を得てこのノートの編集にあたり、巻末に昭和18年9月付けの跋を添え『熊本高校時代に於ける Lafcadio Hearn の英語教授』と題した原稿を作製し、北星堂主の中土義敬に出版を依頼した。時は太平洋戦争の最中である。戦争中の日本では女学校の中には英語教育をなおざりにする学校も出たが、しかし中学、高校、大学などでは引き続き教えていた。昭和19年4月には研究社は岡倉由三郎主幹著の『新英和大辞典』（昭和11年初版）の第 96 版を 28,000 部出しており、ほかならぬ当時中学1年生の私は9円で買い求めている。当時の日本にこれだけの部数の英和辞書の需要があったのであり、心ある人たちは英語教育を軽視していたわけではない。

第2次世界大戦当時までの日本では中学校へ進学する人の割合は平成の今日の大学へ進学する人の割合よりもはるかに低かった。ということはある程度選ばれた若者だけが中学に進んだということである。中学は義務教育ではなく、エリート・コースの一端であった。その関係で、授業水準は平均して高く、教科書の内容は今日よりむしろ充実していた。英語教科書の出版社もいまと違って少なく、しかし出版物の水準は高く、内容はきちんとしていた。その代表的な英語教科書出版社の1つが中土義敬の北星堂だったのである。中土は富山高校の初代校長の南日恒太郎夫人の甥にあたる人で、明治22年生、明治41年富山県立商業学校を出、大正4年北星堂を創立した。英語学者として著名な南日はそんな誼もあってすでに大正5年、英詩文の研究翻訳を収めた『英文藻塩草』『英詩藻塩草』を北星堂から出している。南日に依頼されて富山高校が買い上げたハーンの蔵書を関東大震災の翌々月、洋大箱14個に荷造りして東京から富山へ送り出したのも北星堂だが、しかしそうしたことよりも中土義敬の真に大きな功績は、米国で1922年にホートン・ミフリン社から刊行された全16巻のハーン著作集に洩れた文章を北星堂がそれ以後20年近くさまざまな形で次々に出版したことであろう。北星堂が出したハーンの書物と教科書、ハーン関係の文献については後掲の千田篤氏作成の一覧表を見られたい。当時の北星堂は海外からも高い評価を受けていた。それというのも北星堂は『福翁自伝』の英訳を出版するなど外国向けに日本文化を発信した戦前の数少ない出版社[2]だったからである。

　ところで戦時中の日本では印刷用紙の割当という問題もあり、またそれにあわせて出版統制も行なわれていた。といっても日本の統制は全体主義国に比べればはるかに緩やかなものであった。たとえば北星堂は昭和17年12月にはブライス『禅と英文学』R.H.Blyth, *Zen in English Literature and Oriental Classics* という英国人の著者の手になる英文著書を1,000部出版している。著者のブライスは戦前は金沢の第四高等学校の教授であったが開戦とともに敵国国民として神戸付近に抑留された。それにもかかわらず北星堂は著者との約束を守ったのだから、大した出版社であった。しかし『禅と英文学』に対しては出版許可が出たものの、それから9ヶ月も経つと、戦局が悪化し紙も不足したからであろうか、あるいは内容が特殊と思われたからであろうか、それとも審査委員が変って英語教育を不用とみなしたからであろうか、『熊本高校時代に於ける Lafcadio Hearn の英語教授』の出版は日本出版会の承認するところとならなかった。それで昭和18年秋、中土は高田に原稿を送り返した。しかし返送に先立ち、後日のために考えて、原稿（すなわち高田が編輯した友枝のハーンの英語教授ノート）を全文コピーしたのである。ゼロクスもなく写真撮影もままならぬ時勢であったから、中土はペンで全52ページを学用ノート統制株式会社の大学ノートに筆写したのであった。

---
[2] 次代の中土順平が社長であった昭和32年にも北星堂は阿川弘之『魔の遺産』の John M.Maki の手になる英訳 *Devil's Heritage* を出版して国際ペン大会の参加者全員に献呈している。広島の原子爆弾投下の「魔の遺産」を扱った作品であるが、反響はほとんどなかったと阿川は言っている。

昭和20年8月に日本が降伏しアメリカ軍が進駐するや、日本全土にはにわかに英語学習熱が高まって、英語教育関係の出版は隆盛をきわめた。しかし中土義敬はすでに昭和20年2月に、高田力も昭和21年1月に死去したこともあり、北星堂もまた他の仕事に忙殺されたからであろう、『熊本高校時代に於けるLafcadio Hearnの英語教授』は忘れられたままになっていた。

　その当時は北星堂のベーシック・イングリッシュの教科書などは実によく売れた由である。私も北星堂の英語教科書で多く学び多く教えた。当時はハーンの文章がきわめて多く教材として用いられた。昭和20年代、30年代当時はかつてハーンから直接間接に学んだ英文学教授の影響力が英語教育界に残っていたからでもあろうか。北星堂も代替わりし東大法学部出身の中土順平が2代目として家業を継いでいたが、戦後さらに数十年、北星堂の経営は中土家の手からついに離れることとなった。その際、以前の資料は処分され散逸しかけたが、中土家の親戚で昭和40年代前半に北星堂に寄宿していたことのある富山の公認会計士千田篤氏がそれを惜しみ、その資料を富山大学図書館に送付する仲にたち、届いた資料の整理にあたった。その中に中土義敬が昭和18年に筆写した『熊本高校時代に於けるLafcadio Hearnの英語教授』もはいっていたのを千田氏が見つけたのである。それを見せられたマリ・クリスティーヌ富山大学客員研究員は英語教育の資料として役に立つと思い、トランスクリプションと日本語訳文の作成も試みた。2011年10月富山大学の教養講座に招かれハーンについて講じた平川はその資料を見せられそのハーン研究上の価値に気づき、関係者の注意を促し、先の松江時代の『ラフカディオ・ハーンの英作文教育』に引き続き、この熊本時代の『ラフカディオ・ハーンの英語教育』も同じく福岡の弦書房を通じて刊行することを薦めた。幸い富山大学から便宜を得、かつ富山大学の前身富山高校の初代校長南日恒太郎氏の孫にあたる松井玖美氏からご援助を賜り、出版にこぎつけることを得た次第である。

　大庄屋であった友枝家の明治維新前後の職務上の記録は友枝高彦の先々代友枝多左衛門と先代友枝角之助のいわゆる友枝文書は質量ともに稀に見る貴重な文献で、現在九州大学の九州文化史研究施設に保存されている。大村にあった友枝家の屋敷は広大なものであったが、現在は残っていない。しかし屋敷地の周囲には往時のままの石垣が残り、面影を偲ばせている。友枝の問題のノートはあるいは友枝資料館に保存されているかと期待されたが、2012年2月22日、マリ・クリスティーヌ氏と千田篤氏が友枝の次男の子で陶芸家の友枝觀水氏の付添いで調査したけれども見つからなかった。ただ友枝高彦の明治27年2学期の席次が2番であるという4月25日付の親宛の通知表や東京帝大入学時の写真は見つかった。戦争中友枝高彦は東京都駒込区曙町24(現在は文京区本駒込と地番を改めた)に住んでいたようだが、そのあたりは米国空軍の焼夷弾投下による無差別爆撃で戦災にあったため、高田力からそこへ送り返されたであろうノートは焼失した公算が大である。高田力のコピーもまた現在所在不明である。富山市が1945年8月1日から2日にかけての夜、

アメリカ軍の無差別空爆によって市街地は炎上したが、近くに英国兵捕虜収容所があったために爆撃を免れたという富山高等学校内に住んでいた高田は被災しなかったらしい。

しかし友枝のノート、高田のコピーの再発見が難しい以上、影印版には中土のコピーを復元することとした。英語書物の刊行に特化していた出版人の中土の筆写はきわめて信用度が高いものと考えられるからであり、この機会に優れた出版人の功績を顕彰したいからである。そうした経緯にかんがみ、先人の功をたたえたく思い『ラフカディオ・ハーンの英語教育』の編者として友枝高彦、高田力、中土義敬の3人の故人のお名前を表紙に掲げることとした。

この『ラフカディオ・ハーンの英語教育』は、日本人英語教師のみならず外国人が英語を日本人に教える際にも参考になる記録であろう。そのために監修者平川祐弘が英語の「まえがき」もあわせて執筆した。西川盛雄教授には日本文で本書の内容とその意義について説明をお願いした。西川教授は先に松江時代の『ラフカディオ・ハーンの英作文教育』を編集したハーン研究者であり、この種の仕事の適任者であると信じたからである。

最後に出版助成の件で格別のご配慮いただいた松井玖美様、出版の便宜を計っていただいた富山大学遠藤俊郎学長、マリ・クリスティーヌ研究員、千田篤氏、ヘルン文庫の栗林裕子氏以下教職員各位、先の『ラフカディオ・ハーンの英作文教育』に引き続き『ラフカディオ・ハーンの英語教育』の出版を引き受けた弦書房小野静男氏にお礼申し上げる。

ラフカディオ・ハーンが一番おそれていたことは自分の授業ノートが「それにふさわしくない全く無能な日本人の先生によって」by a totally incompetent Japanese teacher 活字にされることだった、ハーンは心配のあまり文部次官あてに抗議文を書いている。なにしろその手紙が書かれたのが熊本を去った翌年の明治28年5月11日のことであるだけに、ハーンが抗議したことで話題となったノートが英語の授業でなく英文学の授業のノートであったとはいえ、甚だ考えさせられるところが多かった。地下のハーンの霊を怒らせることのない1冊として本書が世に出、広く活用されることを切に祈る次第である。

        平成24年12月15日
        富山大学、ハーン「クレオール日本」シンポジウムの日に

北星堂が出版した小泉八雲関連書籍リスト

(千田篤・作成)

　北星堂は、大正4年、東京市神田区錦町に創立された。当初より、英文を中心とする欧文高等教学図書並びに対外向け日本紹介英文図書の出版を志し、あわせて海外との文化交流に尽力した。第二次世界大戦前は小泉八雲関連の図書出版、戦後にはR.H.ブライスの図書出版、ベイシック・イングリッシュなどの英語教科書出版を盛んに行ない、評判を取った。

　創業初代社長は、中土義敬(なかつちよしたか)(富山県出身、明治22年10月2日〜昭和20年2月15日)である。北星堂はすでに大正9年からハーンの弟子田部隆次、落合貞三郎、大谷正信らが英和対訳本に仕立てたハーンの代表作を広く世に問うことに成功した。

　大正11年、中土義敬は、八雲の死後の遺稿管理者であるM.M.マクドナルドから「君はまだ若い青年である。偉大な文豪の遺著を発行してくれたならば親友であつた私ばかりでなく、雑司ヶ谷の地下に眠るラフカディオもどんなに満足するだろう」との激励を受け、八雲の遺作出版を畢生の使命と決心し精力をかたむけた。ただし以下のリストに挙げられた大部分の書物は全集の中から選ばれて作られた教科書版で学術的価値は高くない。しかし1922年にホートン・ミフリン社(Houghton Mifflin)から出た16巻の全集 The Writings of Lafcadio Hearn に洩れたハーンの手になるロティやゾラ、モーパッサンなど英訳、一連の文学講義、チェンバレンからの書簡、1939年に西崎一郎が編集した5巻本の Lafcadio Hearn's American Articles ならびに Albert Mordell の手で編まれたモーパッサン、ロティ、ゾラなどのフランス文学からのハーンの手になる英訳短篇もの4冊などは海外の新聞等の書評で高く好意的に取り上げられた。英語芸術作品が英語国でなく日本で日の目を見たからである。この中で確実にリプリントに値する1冊は Lafcadio Hearn : On Art, Literature and Philosophy, 1932 であろう。田部、落合、西崎がハーンの東大講義でかつて Erskine が編集した4冊本に洩れた優れた講義をまとめたものの第1冊で、そのほかハーンの東大講義をきちんと出版したことはまことに貴重である。そのような中土は八雲の遺族からも厚い信頼を得た。奇とするに足りるのは1942年にベルタ・フランツォースのドイツ語訳『怪談』を教科書版で出していることで、いいだももは戦時中、第一高等学校で竹山道雄から習った思い出を語っている。

　中土義敬の死後は、甥で養子の中土順平(なかつちじゅんぺい)(富山県出身、大正4年1月11日〜平成17年7月1日)が外地から戻り、二代目社長として出版業を引き継ぎ、焦土の中、東京都千代田区神田錦町で株式会社北星堂書店として再建した。その後順平は体調を崩したが、親族血縁者に事業を引き継ぐ者がいなかったため、昭和59年頃、第三者に事業を譲渡した。

　このたびの講義ノート Lafcadio Hearn's English Lessons は、義敬が戦時中に出版を断念したものであるが、順平の死後に遺品の中から発見された。

　なお、北星堂から出版された八雲関連の出版物は、下記のとおり。

Lafcadio Hearn ; translated and annotated by R. Tanabe
　　Diaries and letters　1920
Lafcadio Hearn ; translated and annotated by T. Ochiai
　　Impressions of Japan　1920
Lafcadio Hearn ; tr. & annot. by M. Otani
　　Letters from Tokyo　1920
Hearn, Lafcadio and 田部隆次
　　『英語教師の日記と手紙』　1920
Lafcadio Hearn ; translated & annotated by M. Otani
　　Insect literature　1921

Lafcadio Hearn ; translated and annotated by R. Tanabe
  Kokoro   1921
Lafcadio Hearn ; translated and annotated by M. Otani
  Sea literature   1921
tr. & annot. by M. Otani ; Lafcadio Hearn
  Island voyages   1922
Lafcadio Hearn ; translated and annotated by T. Ochiai
  On literature   1922
Lafcadio Hearn ; translated and annotated by R. Tanabe
  Kwaidan   1923
Lafcadio Hearn
  Hi-mawari   1924
Hearn, Lafcadio and 落合貞三郎
  Lands and seas   1924
Hearn, Lafcadio and 田部隆次
  Life and literature   1924
Lafcadio Hearn ; compiled with notes by R. Tanabe
  Stories and sketches   1925
Lafcadio Hearn 他；熊野吉次郎編
  TWELVE BEST SHORT STORIES From British and American Writers(HIMAWARI)   1925
Lafcadio Hearn ; compiled, with notes, by R. Tanabe
  Poets and poems   1926
Lafcadio Hearn
  A history of English literature : in a series of lectures   1927
Lafcadio Hearn ; edited by R. Tanabe
  Some strange English literary figures of the eighteenth and nineteenth centuries   1927
Hearn, Lafcadio
  Lafcadio Hearn on Shelley and Keats : from Poets and poems   19--
Lafcadio Hearn
  Supplement to a history of English literature   1927[1927-?]
Lafcadio Hearn 他
  CRTCAL AND MISCELLIANEOUS WRITINGS(Note Upon the Shortest Form of English Poetry)   1928
Lafcadio Hearn ; compiled with notes by T. Ochiai
  Japan and the Japanese   1928
Lafcadio Hearn ; edited by Iwao Inagaki
  Lectures on Shakespeare   1928
Lafcadio Hearn
  Life and Humanity   1928
Lafcadio Hearn 他
  LITERARY PROSES WITH FOOT-NOTES (On Rossetti's "Sea Limits")   1928
Lafcadio Hearn ; compiled with notes by R. Tanabe
  Romance and reason   1928
Lafcadio Hearn.
  Yaizu   1928
Lafcadio Hearn ; with an introduction by Albert Mordell ; edited by Sanki Ichikawa
  Essays on American literature   1929
Lafcadio Hearn ; edited, with notes by R. Tanabe

Facts and fancies　1929
Hokuseido publicatins of the works of Lafcadio Hearn and Glenn W. Shaw
　　1929
Lafcadio Hearn
　　Lectures on prosody　1929
with notes by I. Yamada
　　Select readings from Lafcadio Hearn　1930
Lafcadio Hearn
　　Victorian Philosophy　1930[c1930]
Guy de Maupassant ; translated by Lafcadio Hearn ; with an introd. by Albert Mordell
　　The adventures of Walter Schnaffs and other stories　1931[c1931]
Lafcadio Hearn
　　Athletic contests　1932
Lafcadio Hearn
　　Fuji-no-yama ; The festival of the dead　1932
Lafcadio Hearn ; edited by Ryuji Tanabe, Teisaburo Ochiai and Ichiro Nishizaki
　　On art, literature and philosophy　1932
ラフカディオ・ヘルン作；南日恒太郎著
　　『はかなき契り；新女護島物語』　1932
translated by Lafcadio Hearn ; with an introduction by Albert Mordell.
　　Stories from Pierre Loti　1933
Leona Queyrouze Barel
　　The idyl : my personal reminiscences of Lafcadio Hearn　1933
Lafcadio Hearn ; edited by Ryuji Tanabe and Teisaburo Ochiai ; 3rd edition, rev. by Ichiro Nishizaki and A. Stanton Whitfield
　　A history of English literature　1934
P.D. and Ione Perkins ; with an introduction by Sanki Ichikawa
　　Lafcadio Hearn : a bibliography of his writings　1934
Lafcadio Hearn ; edited by Ryuji Tanabe, Teisaburo Ochiai and Ichiro Nishizaki
　　On poetry　1934
Hearn, Lafcadio and 田部隆次 and 落合貞三郎 and 西崎一郎
　　On poets　1934
Lafcadio Hearn
　　The complete Lafcadio Hearn lectures　1934
高田力著
　　『小泉八雲の横顔』　1934.11
translated by Lafcadio Hearn ; edited with preface by Albert Mordell
　　Sketches and tales from the French　1935.9
translated by Lafcadio Hearn ; edited with preface by Albert Mordell
　　Stories from Emile Zola　1935.9
compiled by Kazuo Koizumi
　　Letters from Basil Hall Chamberlain to Lafcadio Hearn　1936
Kenneth P. Kirkwood
　　Unfamiliar Lafcadio Hearn　1936
丸山学著
　　『小泉八雲新考』　1936.12
compiled by Kazuo Koizumi
　　More letters from Basil Hall Chamberlain to Lafcadio Hearn and letters from M. Toyama, Y.

  Tsubouchi and others 1937
Lafcadio Hearn ; edited by Ichiro Nishizaki
  Barbarous barbers and other stories 1939
Lafcadio Hearn ; edited by Ichiro Nishizaki
  Buying Christmas toys and other essays 1939
Lafcadio Hearn ; edited by Ichiro Nishizaki
  Literary essays 1939
Lafcadio Hearn ; edited by Ichiro Nishizaki
  Oriental articles 1939
edited with an introduction by Ichiro Nishizaki
  Stories of mystery from Lafcadio Hearn 1939
Hearn, Lafcadio and 西崎一郎
  Stories of mystery from Lafcadio Hearn : from "Kwaidan", "Shadowings", "Kotto", etc 1939
Lafcadio Hearn ; edited by Ichiro Nishizaki
  The new radiance and other scientific sketches 1939
[Lafcadio Hearn] ; compiled by Shigetsugu Kishi
  Lafcadio Hearn's Lectures on Tennyson 1941
Hearn, Lafcadio and Franzos, Berta
  Kwaidan und das japanische Lacheln 1942
[compiled by Kazuo Koizumi]
  A drop of dew 1950
田部隆次著
  『小泉八雲：ラフカディオ・ヘルン』 1950.6
Marcel Robert
  Lafcadio Hearn 1950-1951
Hearn, Lafcadio
  Glimpses of unfamiliar Japan (a selection) 1952
Hearn, Lafcadio and 田部隆次
  On composition 1952
Hearn, Lafcadio and 田部隆次
  Otokichi's daruma 1952
Hearn, Lafcadio and 田部隆次
  The dream of a summer day 1952
Hearn, Lafcadio and 田部隆次
  The goblin spider : & other stories 1952
Hearn, Lafcadio and 田部隆次
  The question of the highest arts 1953
[Lafcadio Hearn] ; with notes by R. Tanabe
  Romance of the middle ages 1953.6
Lafcadio Hearn ; a selection edited with notes by Shohei Uchiyama
  Japan : an attempt at interpretation 1958
Frost, O. W.
  Young Hearn 1958
Hearn, Lafcadio and 内山正平
  『日本文化の研究』 1958
edited with notes by Hideo Nakanishi
  Gems from Hearn 1959.8
Lafcadio Hearn ; edited with notes by Makoto Sangu

Editorials from the Kobe Chronicle　1960
Lafcadio Hearn［著］；中西秀男訳注
　Selected stories ＝ハーン名作集　1964.7
Hearn, Lafcadio and 田部隆次
　『人生と文学』　1967
Maupassant, Guy de and Hearn, Lafcadio and 伊丹敬吾
　Short stories by Guy de Maupassant　1969
Hearn, Lafcadio and 田部隆次
　The English romantic poets : Byron, Wordsworth, Shelley & keats　1971
Lafcadio Hearn；edited with notes by Sakae Izumida
　Selected essays of Hearn　1972.1
Hearn, Lafcadio and 角田史郎 and 物部清三
　The best french stories　1974
L. ハーン著；池田雅之編注
　『文学の解釈』　1981.4
L. ハーン著；遠田勝編注
　『日本人の微笑』　1989.12
Lafcadio Hearn；edited with notes by A.D. Rosen, Kiyoshi Fukuzawa, Shigemi Satomi
　Glimpses of unfamiliar Japan　1993
Hearn, Lafcadio and Rosen, A.D.
　『日本のおもかげ』　1993
Lewis, Oscar and Barel, Leona Queyrouze and Kirkwood, Kenneth P.
　Hearn and his biographers . The idyl . Unfamiliar Lafcadio Hearn . Lafcadio Hearn in New Orleans　2008
西川盛雄編著
　『ハーン曼荼羅』　2008.11

Lafcadio Hearn's American articles

Hokuseido Hearn texts
Guy de Maupassant; Translated by Lafcadio Hearn
　Adventures of Walter Schnaffs and Other Stories

注1：リストの作成方針
　富山大学附属図書館の蔵書とCiNii（サイニー：国立情報学研究所Niiのデータベース）から、北星堂及びHokuseidoをキーワードで検索し、その中からハーン関連とおもわれる書籍を抽出し、刊行年順に並べた。それに中土家の遺品で補充した。
注2：Lafcadio Hearn's American articles
　次の5冊である、いずれも1939年刊。これは1992年に東京都文京区本駒込3-22-4の山本雅三が経営する北星堂と雄松堂の手で再刊された。*The new radiance and other scientific sketches ／ Barbarous barbers and other stories ／ Buying Christmas toys and other essays ／ Oriental articles ／ Literary essays*
注3：Hokuseido Hearn texts
　次のものがある。刊行は1953年以後。
　The goblin spider : &other stories ／ From hoki to oki ／ The question of the highest arts ／ Life and literature ／ A journey to Japan ／ Romance of the middle ages ／ Glimpses of unfamiliar Japan (a selection) ／ The dream of a summer day ／ Otokichi's daruma ／ On composition

講義ノート
『熊本高校時代に於ける Lafcadio Hearn の英語教授』
筆写原版・復元・日本語訳

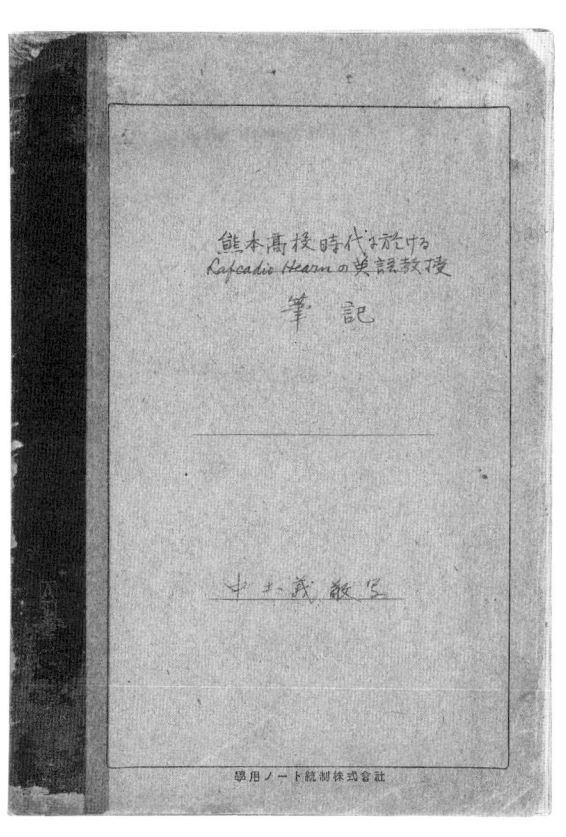

本筆記は富山高校教授宮田力が東京文理大名誉教授友枝高彦氏のノートから轉写され其れに友枝教授の熊本時代の追憶録と宮田氏の「教壇に於けるハ雲先生」といふ前書を添へて出版せんとしたる処「日本出路会」の不承認となりし為、Hearnの講義のみ後日のため写し取り他は宮田教授の手許へ返送したり。次は宮田教授が本書出版にあたり巻末にかへんとした跋の一部である：—

宮田教授：—

「数年前であるが、八雲の熊本第五高等學校時代の生徒であられた私の恩師東京文理大名誉教授友枝高彦先生をヘルン文庫に御案内申上げる機会を得た。その時先生は八雲の講義の筆記帳を未だ保存して居る由を漏らされた。間もなく私は特に御願ひして暫くその筆記帳を拝借することが出来た。私は歡喜と好奇の心で胸をふくらましつヽ、一頁一頁と此の五十年前の文字を判読して行くうちに、八雲が極めて忠実懇篤なる良教師であって、教授を初学者に徹底させるために深甚なる工夫を凝らしてゐた事実を知って、今更の如く驚いたのであった。

八雲の東京帝大に於ける諸種の英文學の講義は、既にその殆と總てのものヽ刊行が遂げられてゐるのであるが、松江中學や熊本五高時代の英語に関する講義筆記で、纏ってヘリにされたものは未だ皆無である。それで、此の筆記の出版を友枝先生に御願ひしたところが、たちどころに賛意を表されて校訂編輯のことを私に委ねられ、且つ序文として五十年前の五高時代の八雲の思出を書いて下さったのである。茲に深く先生に対して感謝を捧げ度いと思ふ。

さて本書の中核を成す八雲の講義は、當時の豫科第三年（其の頃の所謂高等中學校は豫科三年、本科二年であった。）の生徒に對してなされたもので、明治二十六年の秋より翌二十七年

本筆記は富山高校 高田力 教授が東京文理大名誉教授友枝高彦氏のノートから轉寫され其れに友枝教授の熊本時代の追想録と高田氏の「教壇に於ける八雲先生」といふ前書を添へて出版せんとしたるも「日本出版会」の不承認となりし為、Hearnの講義のみ後日のために写し取り他は高田教授の手許へ返送したり。次は高田教授が本書出版にあたり末巻に加へんとした跋の一部である：──

高田教授：──

「数年前であるが、八雲の熊本第五高等學校時代の生徒であられた私の恩師東京文理大名誉教授友枝高彦先生をヘルン文庫に御案内申上げる機会を得た。その節先生は八雲の講義の筆記帳を未だ保存して居る由を洩らされた。間もなく私は特に御願ひして暫くその筆記帳を拝借することが出来た。私は歓喜と好奇の心で胸をふくらましつゝ、一頁一頁と此の五十年前の文字を判読して行くうちに、八雲が極めて忠実懇篤なる良教師であつて、教授を初学者に徹底させるために深甚なる工夫を凝らしてゐた事実を知つて、今更の如く驚いたのであつた。

八雲の東京帝大に於ける諸種の英文學の講義は、既にその殆ど総てのものゝ刊行が遂げられてゐるのであるが、松江中學や熊本五高時代の英語に関する講義筆記で、纏つて公けにされたものは未だ皆無である。それで、此の筆記の出版を友枝先生に御願ひしたところが、たちどころに賛意を表されて校訂編輯のことを私に委ねられ、且つ序文として五十年前の五高時代の八雲の思出を書いて下さつたのである。茲に深く先生に対して感謝を捧げ度いと思ふ。

さて本書の中核を成す八雲の講義は、当時の豫科第三年（其の頃の所謂高等中學校は豫科三年、本科二年であった。）の生徒に對してなされたもので、明治二十六年の秋より翌二十七年

に亘るものである。主として我国の學生の誤り易い語の用法、文法の要点等を或は語源を通し、或はスケッチにより、或は面白い小話を交へて、極めて明快に、印象的に興味深く説明したものである。　教材も空、色、音、風、地震等の天象地異、竹、萱、楠、鳥、蝙蝠等の動植物、或は又郷土を中心とした熊本城、水前寺、太宰府等にも及ぶといふ風で極めて多方面に亘ってゐる。之を要するに、八雲は私が本書の解説として、前著「小泉八雲の横顔」から再録した「教師としての八雲」の中に詳述したやうに、教師として一家の見識を固く持してゐたものであったと思ふ。即ち、彼は生徒の想像力に訴へ、それを働かせて興味深く教へることを教授の要諦と考へたのである。これは動もすれば、無味乾燥で不徹底に流れ易い今日の語学教授に対する立派な一つの抗議となり得るものと思はれる。用例のごときも常に日本人的見地に立って與へられてゐることも注意すべきであって、例へば、明治二十七年三月九日明治天皇御銀婚式奉祝の記念郵便切手に就いての文章があったりするのである。かうした点などは、現今主張せられてゐる新制度に即応した皇国中心の外国語教授の要諦であって、八雲は半世紀前に既にこのことを実行してゐたと言ふことが出来ると思ふ。彼の講義は全体として、科学的であり、且つ文学的であって、今此の講義を公刊して世に送ることは、教壇人に教授上多大の示唆を与へるのみでなく、八雲の人及び藝術に興味を持つ人に盡きざる興味と問題を提供するであらうと思ふのである。

　終りに、本書の編輯について種々助力を与へられた元同僚、現興亜工業大学教授木俣修氏並びに二十数年来諸種のヘルン本の刊行に獻身的努力を捧げて来られ、此の交、快く本書出版の労を引き受けて下さった北豐館主牛土義教氏に対して深く感謝の意を表する次第である。

　　　昭和十八年九月
　　　　富山高等学校ヘルン文庫に於て

　　　　　　　　　　　　　　　　　　　　　　　　葛田　力

に亘るものである。主として我国の學生の誤り易い語の用法、文法の要点等を或は語源を通し、或はスケツチにより、或は面白い小話を交へて、極めて明快に、印象的に興味深く説明したものである。教材も空、色、音、風、地震等の天象地異、竹、藁、棉、鳥、蝙蝠等の動植物、或は又郷土を中心とした熊本城、水前寺、太宰府等にも及ぶといふ風で極めて多方面に亘つてゐる。之を要するに、八雲は私が本書の解説として、前著「小泉八雲の横顔」から再録した「教師としての八雲」の中に詳述したやうに、教師として一家の見識を固く持してゐたものであつたと思ふ。即ち、彼は生徒の想像力に訴へ、それを働かせて興味深く教へることを教授の要諦と考へたのである。これは動もすれば、無味乾燥で不徹底に流れ易い今日の語学教授に対する立派な一つの抗議となり得るものと思はれる。用例のごときも常に日本人的見地に立つて與へられてゐることも注意すべきであつて、例へば、明治二十七年三月九日明治天皇御銀婚式奉祝の記念郵便切手に就いての文章があつたりするのである。かうした点などは、現今主張せられてゐる新制度に即応した皇國中心の外国語教授の要諦であつて、八雲は半世紀前に既にこのことを実行してゐたと言ふことが出来ると思ふ。彼の講義は全体として、科学的であり、且つ文学的であつて、今此の講義を校訂して世に送ることは、教壇人に教授上多大の示唆を与へるのみでなく、八雲の人及び藝術に興味を持つ人に盡きざる興味と問題を提供するであらうと思ふのである。

　終りに、本書の編輯について種々助力を与へられた元同僚、現興亜工業大学教授木俣修氏並びに二十数年来諸種のヘルン本の刊行に献身的努力を捧げて来られ、此の度快く本書出版の労を引き受けて下さつた北星堂主中土義敬氏に対して深く感謝の意を表する次第である。

　　昭和十八年九月
　　　富山高等学校　ヘルン文庫に於て
　　　　　　　　　　　　　　　　高田　力

Lafcadio Hearn の英語教授 (熊本高校時代生徒ニホールニ書イテ渡シタルモノ)

   Each one, in turn, tell me something about the summer vacation — anything curious or interesting or pleasant or beautiful that you saw.

   The more mistakes you make, the better for you, — because we all learn by making mistakes.

   I found that doing nothing was the very hardest kind of work.

   visit = vizʹit = viZʹit

Country

   The word "country" is difficult for you. (You said "I came back to my country".)
   It means in English: —
1. The whole of a country inhabited by one race. "My country" means the whole of Japan.

2. The woods and fields as distinguished from the city. <u>the</u> country = out of the city
Proverb: — "God made the country; but man made the town."

   The English word <u>country</u>, therefore, does not translate the Japanese word <u>Kuni</u>. In speaking of the place where you were born, you must say "my native province"

Lafcadio Hearn の英語教授（熊本高校時代生徒にボードに書いて説明したもの）

    Each one, in turn, tell me something about the summer vacation — anything curious or interesting or pleasant or beautiful that you saw.

    The more mistakes you make, the better for you, — because we all learn by making mistakes.

    I found that doing nothing was the very hardest kind of work.

    visit = víźit = viZ´it

Country

    The word "country" is difficult for you. (You said "I came back to my country".)

    It means in English :－
1. The whole of a country inhabited by one race. "My country" means the whole of Japan.
2. The woods and fields as distinguished from the city. <u>the</u> country = out of the city
Proverb:－"God made the country; but man made the town."

    The English word <u>country</u>, therefore, does not translate the Japanese word <u>Kuni</u>. In speaking of the place where you were born, you must say "my native province"

Lafcadio Hearn の英語教授（熊本高校時代生徒にボードに書いて説明したもの）

各自、順番に夏休みのことを話してください－なにか不思議な、面白い体験をしたり、楽しかったり、美しいものを見たりしたことをです。

英語は間違いをすればするほど、上達します。－なぜなら、間違いをすることで、私たちは学ぶからです。

何もしないこと自体が一番大変な仕事だと分かりました。

    visit = víźit = viZ´it

国、田舎

country という語は難しいです。あなたが今、I came back to my country と言ったとしましょう。

英語でその意味は：－
１．ある民族が暮らす一国全体のこと。「私の国」（My country）とは、日本国全体を指します。
２．都市とは違って森や畑がある地域のこと。<u>the</u> country ＝都市から外れたところ
ことわざ：－神は田園をつくり、人は都市をつくりました。

英語の <u>country</u> は、日本語の生れ故郷を意味する国の訳語とはなりません。生まれた地域のことを話す際には、my native province

or "my home" — but never "my country". "Country" — meaning <u>out of the city</u> — always has **THE** before it.
Examples: — "Is Mr. — at home?"
"No; he has gone into <u>the</u> country."
"Where to?"   "To Aso."

<u>Fune</u>

steamer, steamship } large steamvessel

steamboat — now generally used for a small ship.

<u>gunkan</u> { man-of-war
men-of-war (plural).

<u>Ike</u>

pond { This word is seldom used for any body of fresh running water. When it is so used, it means something very small.

{ The word <u>pool</u> is more often used of fresh water. — Ornamental water in a garden may be called a <u>pond</u>.

or "my home" – but never "my country".
"Country" – meaning <u>out of the city</u> – always has THE before it.
Examples: – "Is Mr.____ at home?"
"No; he has gone into <u>the</u> country."
"Where to?" "To Aso."

とか、my home と言うのであり、my country とはけっして言わないのです。
country －<u>都市から外れたところ</u>を表す場合－はその前にいつも THE をつけます。
例：「○○さんは家にいますか？」
「いいえ、彼は田舎へ行きました。」
「どちらへ行かれましたか？」「阿蘇へ。」

Fune

steamer, steamship, steamvessel } large

steamboat – now generally used for a small ship.

<u>gunkan</u> { man-of-war / men-of-war (plural) }

船

steamer, steamship, steamvessel } 汽船：大型

steamboat － 一般に小型船によく使われる

<u>軍艦</u> { man-of-war / men-of-war (plural)　（複数形） }

Ike

pond { This word is seldom used for any body of fresh running water. When it is so used, it means something very small. }

{ The word <u>pool</u> is more often used of fresh water. – Ornamental water in a garden may be called a <u>pond</u>. }

池

pond（池） { この語は流れている水に使われることはめったにありません。そのように使われるときは、それは非常に小規模のものです。 }

{ pool は同じ池でもたまり水でないきれいなのを指して使われる言葉です。－庭にある造園用の水のたまりを pond といいます。 }

lake — a large enclosed body of fresh water.

Colors

Japanese students make many mistakes at first about the use of words for colors. One reason is that certain Japanese words mean two colors.

Colors are classed as DARK and LIGHT (or BRIGHT)

The sky is <u>bright</u> blue.

What is the color of the uniform (dress) of the students in winter?

It is very <u>dark</u> blue.

Grass is <u>bright</u> (or <u>light</u>) green.

The pine-tree is <u>dark</u> green.

Blood is <u>dark</u> red.

Burning charcoal is <u>bright</u> red.

The skin of the lips is <u>light</u> red. (This kind of red is called PINK.)

Gold is <u>bright</u> yellow.

lake — a large enclosed body of fresh water.

Colors

Japanese students make many mistakes at first about the use of words for colors. One reason is that certain Japanese words mean two colors.

Colors are classed as DARK and LIGHT (or BRIGHT)

The sky is <u>bright</u> blue.

What is the color of the uniform (dress) of the students in winter?

It is very <u>dark</u> blue.

Grass is <u>bright</u> (or <u>light</u>) green.

The pine-tree is <u>dark</u> green.

Blood is <u>dark</u> red.

Burning charcoal is <u>bright</u> red.

The skin of the lips is <u>light</u> red. (This kind of red is called PINK.)

Gold is <u>bright</u> yellow.

lake（湖）－周囲が囲われている真水のひろがり。

色

日本人学生は、はじめは色にまつわる語彙の使用方法でよく間違えます。その原因の1つに、日本語は1つの言葉で2つの色合いを示すことが挙げられます。
色は、DARK（暗色）とLIGHTまたはBRIGHT（明色）に分けられます。
空は、明るい青色です。

冬用の学生服の色は何色ですか？
紺色です。

草は明るい緑色です。

松の木は、深緑色です。

血液は、濃い赤色です。

燃え盛っている炭は明るい赤です。

唇はほんのり明るい赤色です。（この種の赤は、ピンクといいます。）

金は明るい黄色です。

Fire (the flame) is yellow also; and even the light of our sun is somewhat yellow. Yellow is thus the most splendid of all colors.

Dark yellow is usually called brown, — or brownish yellow.

There is a very beautiful color, — partly yellow and partly red. What is it called?

Orange.

Grey (also spelled gray) is the name usually given to the color of stone. The facing of this building is of light grey stone; but we often see stones nearly BLACK, which we call dark-grey or IRON-GREY. Grey is also the color of an old man's hair. The walls of this room are a bluish-grey. We use mixed names for some mixed colors.

greyish - green	When two colors are mixed
greenish - grey	the color which is stronger
greenish - blue	gives the name.
yellowish - brown	
brownish - yellow	

Fine differences in color are called SHADES or TINTS. For instance, the color of the class-book, and of the grass are <u>light</u> green. But the difference

Fire (the flame) is yellow also; and even the light of our sun is somewhat yellow. Yellow is thus the most splendid of all colors.
Dark yellow is usually called brown, – or brownish yellow.

There is a very beautiful color, – partly yellow and partly red. What is it called?
Orange.

Grey (also spelled gray) is the name usually given to the color of stone. The facing of this building is of light grey stone; but we often see stones nearly BLACK, which we call dark-grey or IRON-GREY. Grey is also the color of an old man's hair. The walls of this room are a bluish-grey. We use mixed names for some mixed colors.

grayish-green greenish-grey greenish-blue yellowish-brown brownish-yellow	When two colors are mixed the color which is stronger gives the name.

Fine differences is* color are called SHADES or TINTS. For instance, the color of the class-book, and of the grass are <u>light</u> green. But the difference

* ノートにis とあるが in の誤りであろう。

火（炎）もまた黄色です。太陽の光もやや黄色に近い色ですね。黄色は、このようにすべての色の中で一番すばらしい色です。
暗い黄色は、通常茶色、もしくは茶色がかった黄色と呼ばれています。
非常に美しい色で、半ば黄色で半ば赤の色があります。これを何と言いますか？
オレンジ色。
灰色（grey は gray とも綴られます）は通常、石の色に使われることが多いです。この建物の表面は、明るい灰色の石ですが、私たちがしばしば見かける石は黒（BLACK）に近い。それはダークグレイ（dark-grey）とか鉄灰色（IRON-GREY）と呼びます。灰色は、お年寄りの髪の色です。
この部屋の壁は青みがかった灰色です。
ある種の混合色を表現するには、色名が混ざり合った名称を使用します。

灰色がかった緑 緑がかったグレイ 緑がかった青 黄色がかった茶色 茶色がかった黄色	二つの色が混じり合わさっている時は、強いほうの色が、色の名前となります。

色の微妙なちがいは、SHADES（明暗）とか TINTS（色調）と呼ばれます。
例えば、出欠簿と草の色は、どちらも<u>明るい</u>緑色です。しかし、色の明暗の違いは、

in shade is very great. One is a DEAD green, and the other a WARM green. Unpolished gold is called DEAD gold.

Trees, Plants, Vegetables, Grass, &c.

— Please remember that in conversation these words have NOT the same meaning exactly as in scientific books. For example, the word "vegetable" refers only to food, &c.

1 = Ki — a tree
2 = Ki — wood

We cannot say 'a table is made of tree;' — that would be wrong; we say 'it is made of WOOD.'

Why? — Because WOOD is only the HARD part of a tree. It is the body of a dead tree.

Now has the word WOOD any other meaning?
Yes, it also means a FOREST. A place where many thousands of trees grow together.

Examples: —
Bears (Kuma) live in the WOODS.
He lost his way in a wood.

What is grass? What shape has it?

in shade is very great. One is a DEAD green, and the other a WARM green. Unpolished gold is called DEAD gold.

Trees, Plants, Vegetables, Grass, &c.

— Please remember that in conversation these words have NOT the same meaning exactly as in scientific books. For example, the word "vegetable" refers only to food, &c.

    1 = ki – a tree
    2 = ki – wood

We cannot say 'a table is made of tree'; – that would be wrong; we say 'it is made of WOOD.'
Why? – Because WOOD is only the HARD part of a tree. It is the body of a dead tree.

    Now has the word WOOD any other meaning?
    Yes, it also means a FOREST. A place where many thousands of trees grow together.

Examples :–
    Bears (Kuma) live in the WOODS.
    He lost his way in a wood.

What is grass? What shape has it?

とても大きいです。一方は DEAD（鈍い）緑色なのに対し、他方は WARM（暖かな）緑色です。
研磨されていない金は、DEAD gold（鈍い金色）と言われます。

木、植物、野菜、草など

－覚えていてほしいことは、会話ではこういった語は科学書の場合とは厳密に同じ意味を持たない（NOT）ということです。
例えば、vegetable という語は食べ物にしか使われません。

    1 = ki – a tree（木）
    2 = ki – wood（材木）

「テーブルは tree（立木）でできている」とは言いません。－それは間違いです。「テーブルは wood（材木）でできている」と言います。
どうしてでしょうか？－なぜなら、WOOD は、木の固い（HARD）部分を表すからです。伐採された木の幹のことだからです。
では、WOOD には他の意味もありますか？
森（FOREST）の意味もあります。森は何千もの木がともに成長する場所です。

例－
熊は、森（WOODS）に住んでいる。
彼は、森で道に迷った。

草とは何ですか？　どんな形をしていますか？

Grass is a wild plant that covers the ground. Its leaves are sharp and long.— They are not called leaves, but BLADES because they are shaped like sword-blades. It has no flower.

This is grass.

What is the difference between a PLANT and a TREE?

A tree contains wood; it is hard. A plant generally has no wood; and is soft. A pine is a tree. The <u>tamana</u> (cabbage) is a plant. And many plants die in winter, but trees live.

What do you mean by VEGETABLES?

In conversation the word means only particular plants which are cooked for food, — such as radishes (daikon), potatoes (imo), cabbage (tamana), &c.

But all plants which are cooked for food are not vegetables. Rice, wheat, rye, barley, and corn are never called vegetables;— they are called GRAINS. (CEREALS — scientific or poetical).

Grass is a wild plant that covers the ground. Its leaves are sharp and long. — They are not called leaves, but BLADES because they are shaped like sword-blades. It has no flower.

This is grass.

What is the difference between a PLANT and a TREE?

A tree contains wood; it is hard. A plant generally has no wood; and is soft. A pine is a tree. The <u>tamana</u> (cabbage) is a plant. And many plants die in winter, but trees live.

What do you mean by VEGETABLES?

In conversation the word means only particular plants which are cooked for food, — such as radishes (daikon), potatoes (imo), cabbage (tamana), &c.

But all plants which are cooked for food are not vegetables. Rice, wheat, rye, barley, and corn are never called vegetables; — they are called GRAINS. (CEREALS — scientific or poetical).

草は地面を覆う野生の植物です。その葉は長く先が尖っています。—それは leaves（葉）とは呼ばれません。その形から BLADES（刀身状の葉）と呼ばれます。
そして花をつけることはありません。

これが草です。

PLANT と　TREE の違いは何でしょう。

tree（立木）は wood（材木）を含んでいます。tree が固いのに対し、plant（植物）は wood の部分がなく、柔らかいのです。
松は tree（立木）です。玉菜（キャベツ）は plant（植物）です。多くの plants は冬には枯れますが、tree は生き延びます。

VEGETABLES（野菜）とはどのような意味ですか。

会話の中では vegetables とは、食材のための植物—ラディッシュ（大根）、ポテト（いも）、キャベツ（玉菜）などを指します。
しかし、食材のための植物すべてが vegetables とは限りません。米、小麦、ライ麦、大麦、そしてトウモロコシは vegetables とは言わず、これらは GRAINS（穀物）（科学的、詩的には穀類 CEREALS）と言います。

Do trees give us anything to eat? — Yes, they give us what are called FRUITS (not vegetables), — oranges, pears, peaches, &c.

Very, very small trees of certain kinds are not called trees, although they have a little wood. These are called SHRUBS. There are many shrubs in the garden.

HERBS is a general name for wild plants which are useful for medicine or cooking, or other purposes.

Vegetables is used only of plants cultivated by man.

To give the names of various kinds of wood, first we give the name of the tree — thus, pine-wood, cedar-wood, maple-wood, &c.

"Dog days" —— In England and America the hottest time of the summer is called the dog-days; and some people think the reason is because dogs go mad at that season. But this is not true. The real reason is very ancient. The great star Sirius, which is a sun thousands of times larger than our sun, was called by the ancients the Dog-star, we still call it so. The reason why the ancients called it the Dog-star was that it formed

Do trees give us anything to eat? — Yes, they give us what are called FRUITS (not vegetables), — oranges, pears, peaches, &c.

Very, very small trees of certain kinds are not called trees, although they have a little wood. These are called SHRUBS. There are many shrubs in the garden.

HERBS is a general name for wild plants which are useful for medicine or cooking, or other purposes.

Vegetables is used only of plants cultivated by man.

To give the names of various kinds of wood, first we give the name of the tree — thus, pine-wood, cedar-wood, maple-wood, &c.

"Dog days"— In England and America the hottest time of the summer is called the dog-days; and some people think the reason is because dogs go mad at that season. But this is not true. The real reason is very ancient. The great star Sirius, which is a sun thousands of times larger than our sun, was called by the ancients the Dog-star, we still call it so. The reason why the ancients called it the Dog-star was that it formed

tree は食べ物を私たちに恵んでくれますか？―その通り、木は FRUITS 果物（vegetables ではない）を恵んでくれます、―オレンジや梨や桃など。

極めて小さい trees はほんの僅かばかりの woods があるにしても、tree とは呼びません。これらは、SHRUBS（灌木）と言います。庭には多くの灌木があります。

ハーブ（HERBS）は、薬、料理、その他の目的で利用される野生の植物の一般名です。

vegetables は人が栽培する植物に対してのみ使われる名です。

いろいろな材木（wood）の名前には、まず木（tree）の名前をつけます。―かくして松の材木、杉の材木、かえでの材木などができてきます。

Dog days（土用）―イギリス、アメリカでは、夏の最も暑い時期は dog-days と呼ばれています。犬が狂ってしまうほど暑い季節であることから来た言葉であると考える人もいます。しかし、これは違います。真の理由は古代に遡ります。太陽より数千倍もの大きさを持つシリウスという巨星を古代人は Dog-star（天狼星）と呼んでいました。今も現代人はそう呼んでいます。古代人が Dog-star という言い方をしていたのには、それなりの理由がありました。

part of a number of stars which in the sky had a shape (they thought) like the shape of a dog. In a map of the sky, you will see also a Bear, and a Lion, and many other shapes of animals.

Well, at a certain time in summer the ancients saw that the Dog-star Sirius rose at the same time as our sun in the sky. Then they said:— "that must be what makes it so hot." And they called those hot days the Days of the dog-star Sirius; we call them the Dog-days.

In different ages and different countries the Dog-days begin at different times. In North America they begin on July 25th, and end on September 5th. Some of the names of the stars are Arabian, some Greek, and some Latin. Sirius comes from a Greek word meaning "scorching", "burning hot."

Sounds

Sounds are spoken of as LOUD and LOW. Give an example of a loud sound and a low sound.
The sound of cannon is loud.
The humming of bees is a low sound.
Sounds are called HIGH and DEEP.
Thunder is a DEEP sound and the sound

part of a number of stars which in the sky had a shape (they thought) like the shape of a dog. In a map of the sky, you will see also a Bear, and a Lion, and many other shapes of animals.

Well, at a certain time in summer the ancients saw that the Dog-star Sirius rose at the same time as our sun in the sky. Then they said: — "that must be what makes it so hot." And they called those hot days the Days of the dog-star Sirius; we call them the <u>Dog-days</u>.

In different ages and different countries the Dog-days begin at different times. In North America they begin on July 25th, and end on September 5th. Some of the names of the stars are Arabian, some Greek, and some Latin. Sirius comes from a Greek word meaning "scorching", "burning hot."

Sounds

Sounds are spoken of as LOUD and LOW. Give an example of a loud sound and a low sound.

The sound of cannon is loud.

The humming of bees is a low sound.

Sounds are called HIGH and DEEP.

Thunder is a DEEP sound and the sound

それは、この星は空に星が集まって犬の形をつくる（と古代人が考えた）いくつかの星の一つと考えたからでした。天体図の中に「熊」や「獅子」、その他多くの動物の形をした星座を見つけることができます。

さて、夏のある時期、古代人は Dog-star のシリウスが空に太陽と同時に上がるのを見ました。

そして、こう言いました。「だからこんなに暑いんだ。」それ以後、とても暑い日のことを dog-star シリウスの日と呼ぶようになりました。そして、現代人の我々も <u>Dog-days</u> と呼んでいます。

Dog-days は時代や地域によって始まる時期が異なります。北米では7月25日に始まり、9月5日に終わります。星の名前の中には、アラビア語、ギリシャ語、ラテン語のものがあります。シリウスは「焦がす」「焼き尽くすほど暑い」という意味のギリシャ語に由来しています。

音

音は LOUD（大きい）、LOW（低い）で表します。LOUD と LOW の使い方の例を挙げてください。

大砲の音は大きい（loud）です。

ミツバチのブンブンと唸る音は低い（low）音です。

音には HIGH（<u>高い</u>）と DEEP（<u>深い</u>）があります。

雷は DEEP（太い）音であり、そして

of the trumpet is a HIGH sound. Why do we say DEEP? —— All sounds which are both low and powerful are sounds which seem to shake the ground like the force of waves in a storm. Some men's voices are called DEEP.

Sounds which are very HIGH and also very powerful are called SHRILL. The sound made by sparrows and by <u>semi</u>, and the sound of a steam-whistle on an engine are all SHRILL.

Sounds are called HARSH and SWEET. Disagreeable noises are called HARSH. The sound of a flute and the voices (sometimes) of children and women are called SWEET. But the word SWEET may also be used for some deep sounds —— such as the tones of a fine bell.

There are sounds still HIGHER than shrill sounds, —— which hurt the ears; we call such sounds KEEN and SHARP —— as if we were talking of knives or needles.

Sounds are also called DEAD and DULL. These are sounds that do not ring, that do not make echoes. They do not travel. Striking a log of wood makes such a sound.

There was once a peasant (hyakusho). He had a pet fox, a goose, and a bag of rice. He wanted to take them all across a very wide river. But there was only one very small boat. It was

of the trumpet is a HIGH sound. Why do we say
DEEP? — All sounds which are both low
and powerful are sounds which seem to shake
the ground like the force of waves in a storm.
Some men's voices are called DEEP.

    Sounds which are very HIGH and also very
powerful are called SHRILL. The sound made
by sparrows and by <u>semi</u>, and the sound of
a steam-whistle on an engine are all SHRILL.
    Sounds are called HARSH and SWEET.
Disagreeable noises are called HARSH. The
sound of a flute and the voices (sometimes)
of children and women are called SWEET.
But the word SWEET may also be used for some
deep sounds — such as the tones of a fine
bell.
    There are sounds still HIGHER than shrill
sounds, — which hurt the ears; we call
such sounds KEEN and SHARP — as if we were
talking of knives or needles.

    Sounds are also called DEAD and DULL. These
are sounds that do not ring, that do not make echoes.
They do not travel. Striking a log of wood makes
such a sound.

    There was once a peasant (hyakusho). He had
a pet fox, a goose, and a bag of rice. He
wanted to take them all across a very wide river.
But there was only one very small boat. It was

トランペットの音は HIGH（高い）音です。
なぜ、DEEP というのでしょう？ — 低くて
力強い音はすべて嵐の中の大波に似て、大地
を揺るがすような音だからです。男性の中に
は、その声が DEEP（深みのある）と呼ば
れる人もいます。
とても高く（HIGH）て力強い音は SHRILL
（甲高い）と表現します。雀や蟬の鳴き声、
蒸気機関車の汽笛もすべて SHRILL です。

音は、HARSH、SWEET と形容し、耳障り
な音を HARSH と表現します。フルートの
音や、ときには子どもや女性の声を SWEET
（甘美）といいます。しかし、SWEET とい
う語は、ほかにも何か深い音 — 例えば美し
い鐘の響きのような音 — にも用いられます。

甲高い音よりさらに高い耳をつんざくような
音も存在します。— それはまるでナイフか針
について話すかのようですが、そんな音を
KEEN（耳がキーンとする）とか SHARP（金
切声）と表現します。
音は、DEAD（死んだ音）とか DULL（鈍
い音）とも表現します。これは、響かない、
こだましない音のことです。これらの音は、
遠くまで届きません。丸太をたたくときに、
このような音が出ます。
昔ある所に農夫（百姓）がいました。農夫は
お気に入りの狐や鷲鳥を連れ、米袋を携えて
いました。彼はとても幅の広い川の向こう岸
まで、これらをすべて持って渡りたいと思い
ました。しかし、そこにはとても小さな舟一
艘しかありませんでした。

so small that he could take over only one thing at a time. So he did not know what to do. Because, if he took over the fox first, and then the goose, he knew that the fox would eat the goose. And if he took over the goose first, and then the rice, he knew the goose would eat the rice. So what did he do?

He first took over the goose. Then he took over the fox and brought back the goose. Then he took over the rice, and finally took over the goose again.

Takai

Takai ——— in English this word has several meanings.

A mountain is HIGH.
A person is TALL.

Note: — If we speak of a person as HIGH, we do not mean he is tall, but only that he has great rank and honor. — "The prince is a HIGH personage."

(Carnivorous — flesh-eating, Latin carnis,
What is the opposite of high? — Low. "flesh")
What is the opposite of tall? — Short.
When we say "a low man" we mean a bad (wicked or vulgar (gehin-na)) man.

so small that he could take over only one thing at a time. So he did not know what to do. Because, if he took over the fox first, and then the goose, he knew that the fox would eat the goose. And if he took over the goose first, and then the rice, he knew the goose would eat the rice. So what did he do?

 He first took over the goose. Then he took over the fox and brought back the goose. Then he took over the rice, and finally took over the goose again.

Takai

<u>Takai</u> – in English this word has several meanings.

A mountain is HIGH.
A person is TALL.

Note: – If we speak of a person as HIGH, we do not mean he is tall, but only that he has great rank and honor. – "The prince is a HIGH personage."
 (Carnivorous – flesh-eating, Latin carnis, "flesh".
What is the opposite of high? – Low.
What is the opposite of tall? – Short.
When we say "a low man" we mean a bad (wicked or vulgar (gehin-na)) man.

高い

あまりに小さいので、どれか一つしか舟に乗せることができませんでした。彼はどうすればいいのか、わかりませんでした。なぜなら、もし最初に狐を、次に鵞鳥を連れて行ったら、狐は鵞鳥を食べてしまうことがわかっていたからです。もし、鵞鳥を先に連れて行き、そのあとでお米を持って行ったら、今度は鵞鳥がお米を食べてしまうことがわかっていたからです。彼はどうしたのでしょうか？
彼は、最初に鵞鳥を連れて行きました。そして、狐を連れて行き、鵞鳥を連れ戻しました。そのあとで、お米を運び、最後にもう一度鵞鳥を連れて行ったのでした。

高い：英語ではこの語にはいくつかの意味があります。
「山が高い」は HIGH
「人の背が高い」は TALL

注：－もし人に対して HIGH を使うのであれば、それは背が高いではなく、地位や名誉があるということを意味します。－「王子は身分の高い方です。」
（carnivorous－肉食のこと。ラテン語で carnis は肉、英語の flesh）。
「high の反対は何？」－「Low」（低い）
「tall の反対は何？」－「Short」（背が低い）
a low man（下劣な人）と言うとき、これは悪い（意地悪な、もしくは無作法な（下品な））人という意味になります。

high / low } things   tall / short } persons

A SHORT man may be broad and heavy, so that we cannot call him small.

Note this :—— In English we scarcely ever use the word BODY —— except in the meaning of a dead body, a corpse —— we describe persons in a different way.
A man may be well-built.
strongly-built.
lightly-built.
heavily-built.
slenderly-built.
awkwardly-built.
clumsily-built.
gracefully-built.
powerfully-built.
finely-built.
feebly-built.

The noun "build" is also used in this sense.
Ex.—— "a man of strong build," "a man of very slender build."

The word "knit", meaning knotted or tied together, is also used,—— as "a well-knit

$\left.\begin{array}{l}\text{high}\\\text{low}\end{array}\right\}$ things $\left.\begin{array}{l}\text{tall}\\\text{short}\end{array}\right\}$ persons

$\left.\begin{array}{l}\text{high}\\\text{low}\end{array}\right\}$ 物に用いる語 $\left.\begin{array}{l}\text{tall}\\\text{short}\end{array}\right\}$ 人に用いる語

A SHORT man may be broad and heavy, so that we cannot call him small.

SHORT man というと、恰幅がよく体重の重い人かもしれないので、その人を small ということはできません。

Note this : — In English we scarcely ever use the word BODY — except in the meaning of a dead body, a corpse — we describe persons in a different way.

次のことに注意 : — 英語では、BODY という語はほとんど使いません（死体の意味で用いる場合以外）。人の外見（体格）を述べる仕方はいろいろあります。人間はたとえば次のような体格をしている場合がある。

A man may be <u>well-built</u>.
    <u>strongly-built</u>.
    <u>lightly-built</u>.
    <u>heavily-built</u>.
    <u>slenderly-built</u>.
    <u>awkwardly-built</u>.
    <u>clumsily-built</u>.
    <u>gracefully-built</u>.
    <u>powerfully-built</u>.
    <u>finely-built</u>.
    <u>feebly-built</u>.

<u>いい体格</u>
<u>頑強そうな体格</u>
<u>きゃしゃな体格</u>
<u>どっしりした体格</u>
<u>すらっとした体格</u>
<u>不格好な体格</u>
<u>みっともない体格</u>
<u>しなやかな体格</u>
<u>筋骨たくましい体格</u>
<u>ほっそりと繊細な体格</u>
<u>弱々しい体格</u>

The noun "build" is also used in this sense. Ex. — "a man of strong build," "a man of very slender build."

build が名詞で、この意味で用いられる場合。例 : — a man of strong build（強靭な体格の人）、a man of very slender build（とてもすらりとした体格の人）

The word "knit", meaning <u>knotted</u> or <u>tied together</u>, is also used, — as "a well-knit

knit という語は、「結びつける」「つなげる」という意味であり、次のようにも用いられます。a well-knit man：体の引き締まった人

man." And lastly the word "made" can be used,— as "a well-made man."

<u>Hone to Kawa</u> (Eng. idiom — skin and bone)

A person who is all skin and bone is called very THIN. The opposite of THIN is FAT. In English conversation, however, we do not call people FAT or THIN. We say "stout" instead of "fat", and "slight" or "slender" instead of "thin"; this is merely politeness.

The most beautiful of all these words is GRACEFUL. But it can seldom be used. It does not mean beautiful (or pretty), but something much better.

A bamboo is very light, very slender, very strong, and very flexible. A person who is light, slender, and strong is GRACEFUL. Gracefulness means "the economy of force,"— that is, the greatest possible strength with the least possible weight.

A bamboo is graceful.
A deer is graceful.
A very fine horse is graceful.
A willow is graceful.

man." And lastly the word "made" can be used, — as "a well-made man."

<u>Hone to Kawa</u> (Eng. idiom — skin and bone)

A person who is all skin and bone is called very THIN. The opposite of THIN is FAT. In English conversation, however, we do not call people FAT or THIN. We say "stout" instead of "fat", and "slight" or "slender" instead of "thin"; this is merely politeness.

The most beautiful of all these words is GRACEFUL. But it can seldom be used. It does not mean beautiful (or pretty), but something much better.

A bamboo is very light, very slender, very strong, and very flexible. A person who is light, slender, and strong is GRACEFUL. Gracefulness means "the economy of force," — that is, the greatest possible strength with the best possible weight.

A bamboo is graceful.
A deer is graceful.
A very fine horse is graceful.
A willow is graceful.

made という語は次のように使われます。
a well-made man：しっかりした体つきの人

骨と皮（英語慣用句では skin and bone）

骨と皮ばかりの人のことを、THIN（とても痩せている）と表現します。THIN の反対は、FAT（肥っている）です。しかし、会話では相手に向かって FAT とか THIN とは言いません。fat ではなく stout を、thin ではなく slight とか slender と言います。これが丁寧な言い方です。
こうした語の中で最も美しい語は、GRACEFUL です。しかし、これはめったに使われることのない語です。美しい（あるいはかわいらしい）という意味ではなく、もっとはるかに優れたものを表します。
竹はとても軽く、細く、強く、曲がりやすいものです。軽くて、しなやかで、強靭な人のことを GRACEFUL と表現します。gracefulness とは、「力の効率的使用」、すなわち、体重を最適にして最大の力を発揮できることを意味します。

竹はしなやかです。
鹿は軽快です。
駿馬は優美です。
柳はしなやかです。

Climate and Weather

Climate is the constant condition of the air in a zone, region or country. (from the Greek word _klima_, "a belt," "a girdle" (obi), "a zone" —— a region of the world.)

Climate never changes.

Weather (always changes) (from the ancient German word wetar (storm).) Weather is the condition of the air about us every day. Rain, sunshine, heat, cold, frost, hail, snow, fog, damp, mist, wind —— all these are changes of weather.

Wind

Wind is air in motion.

Breeze —— "a soft or gentle wind."

Gale —— "a very strong wind." (from a Danish word _gal_ meaning "mad.")

Storm (from a Sanskrit word _stur_ meaning "to scatter", "to throw down.")

A very great storm in the Indian Ocean, in the Sea of Japan, or in the China Sea is called a _typhoon_. This word is delivered from the Chinese _tō fung_ (Japanese taifū), —— but it is spelled curiously. Why? —— Because the ancient Greeks had a God of storms called Typhon. When the

Climate and Weather

Climate is the constant condition of the air in a zone, region or country. (from the Greek word klima, "a belt," "a girdle" (obi), "a zone" — a region of the world.)

Climate never changes.

Weather (always changes) (from the ancient German word wetar (storm).) Weather is the condition of the air about us every day. Rain, sunshine, heat, cold, frost, hail, snow, fog, damp, mist, wind — all these are changes of weather.

Wind

Wind is air in motion.

Breeze – "a soft or gentle wind."

Gale – "a very strong wind." (from a Danish word gal meaning "mad.")

Storm (from a Sanskrit word Stur meaning "to scatter," "to throw down.")

A very great storm in the Indian Ocean, in the Sea of Japan, or in the China Sea is called a typhoon. This word is delivered from the Chinese to fung (Japanese taifū), — but it is spelled curiously Why?— Because the ancient Greeks had a God of storms called Typhon. When the

気候と天候

climate は、一区域、地域、国における、一定の大気の状態のことを意味します。（ギリシャ語では klima といい、a belt「地帯」、a girdle「帯」、a zone「地域」のことで、—世界中の一地域のこと）

climate（気候）は決して変化することはありません。

weather（常に変わるもの。古代ゲルマン語の wetar（嵐）から派生した）天候とは、日々の我々の周囲の大気の状態です。雨、晴れ、暑さ、寒さ、霜に霰、雪、濃霧、湿気や霧、風といったこれらのすべてが、天候の変化によるものです。

風

風とは空気（大気）の動きです。

Breeze（そよかぜ）–「柔らかい、おだやかな風」

Gale（疾風、強風）–「とてもつよい風」（デンマーク語の gal から派生。「気が狂った」という意味がある。）

Storm（嵐）（サンスクリット語の Stur から派生。「散らす」「投げ倒す」という意味がある。）

インド洋や日本近海、中国近海で発生する最も規模の大きい嵐のことを、typhoon（台風）といいます。この語は、中国語の to fung* から派生しています（日本語では台風という）。— この単語のつづりは大変興味深いといえます。どうしてでしょう？— 古代ギリシャ人には Typhon と呼ばれた嵐の神がいたからです。

---

*　ピンインで書くと dà fēng となる「大風」の南方方言。

first English sailors went to China and heard the Chinese say <u>to fung</u>, they thought the Chinese word was the same as the Greek one, — so they spelled it in nearly the same way.

Verbs used in speaking of wind and storm.
The wind <u>blows</u>.
It blows OFF (or AWAY) men's hats.
It blows DOWN houses.
It carries AWAY the leaves of the tree.
The wind also makes strange, or terrible, or ghostly noises (storm).
Sometimes it whistles.
Sometimes it wails.
Sometimes it moans.
Sometimes it whispers — as if telling secrets.
Sometimes it murmurs.
Sometimes it roars.
Sometimes it shrieks.
So you see that in English we speak of the wind as if it were a person — or at least as if it were alive.
We also say that it BREATHES.
Ex. — "I felt the pleasant wind breathe upon me."
"To-day there is not a breathe of air."

(to lecture us = to blame us severely — to scold us.
to lecture to us = to teach by an address, etc.)

first English sailors went to China and heard the Chinese say to fung, they thought the Chinese word was the same as the Greek one, — so they spelled it in nearly the same way.

  Verbs used in speaking of wind and storm.
   The wind blows.
   It blows OFF (or AWAY) men's hats.
   It blows DOWN houses.
   It carries AWAY the leaves of the tree.
  The wind also makes strange, or terrible, or ghostly noises (storm).
   Sometimes it whistles.
   Sometimes it wails.
   Sometimes it moans.
   Sometimes it whispers — as if telling secrets.
   Sometimes it murmurs.
   Sometimes it roars.
   Sometimes it shrieks.
  So you see that in English we speak of the wind as if it were a person — or at least as if it were alive.
  We also say that it BREATHES.
  Ex. — "I felt the pleasant wind breathe upon me."
   "To-day there is not a breath* of air."

$$\left(\begin{array}{l} \text{to lecture us = to blame us severely — to scold us.} \\ \text{to lecture to us = to teach by an address, etc.} \end{array} \right)$$

* ノートに breathe とあるが breath の誤りであろう。

Birds

A bird is a creature which flies. But so do insects and other creatures. What is the difference between an insect and a bird? A bird flies high. So does a bat. What is the difference between a bird and a bat? A bat has wings covered with skin,⎯ and a bat's body is covered with fur. But a bird's body is covered with feathers. In English the word "feather" never means a wing.

Do bats lay eggs? A bat does not lay eggs, and it feeds its young with milk. Therefore a bat is a mammal. All creatures which give milk to their young are mammals.
(mammal⎯ from the Latin <u>mamma</u>, "a breast" which gives milk.) Consequently all milk-giving animals are classed as mammalia or mammals.

Do all birds fly? No, some birds cannot fly at all. The ostrich, the emu, the cassowary, and many kinds of marine birds cannot fly. The ostrich can run, however, faster than any other creature. The moa which has become extinct,⎯ a New Zealand bird was from 17 to 20 feet high.

What is the difference between the mouth of a bird and the mouth of a bat? A bat has teeth, a bird has no teeth; and its mouth

Birds

A bird is a creature which flies. But so do insects and other creatures. What is the difference between an insect and a bird? A bird flies high. So does a bat. What is the difference between a bird and a bat? A bat has wings covered with skin, – and a bat's body is covered with fur. But a bird's body is covered with feathers. In English the word "feather" never means a wing.

Do bats lay eggs? A bat does not lay eggs, and it feeds its young with milk. Therefore a bat is a mammal. All creatures which give milk to their young are mammals. (mammal – from the Latin mamma, "a breast" which gives milk.) Consequently all milk-giving animals are classed as mammalia or mammals.

Do all birds fly? No, some birds cannot fly at all. The ostrich, the emu, the cassowary, and many kinds of marine birds cannot fly. The ostrich can run, however, faster than any other creature. The moa which has become extinct, – a New Zealand bird was from 17 to 20 feet high.

What is the difference between the mouth of a bird and the mouth of a bat? A bat has teeth, a bird has no teeth; and its mouth

鳥

鳥は飛ぶ生き物です。しかし、昆虫、そのほかにも飛ぶことが可能な生き物はいます。昆虫と鳥のちがいは何でしょうか。鳥は空高く飛ぶことができます。蝙蝠もそうです。鳥と蝙蝠のちがいは何でしょうか。蝙蝠には地肌で覆われている翼があり、—体は柔毛で覆われています。しかし、鳥の体は、羽毛で覆われています。英語でいう feather は、決して翼を意味するのではありません。

蝙蝠は卵を産むでしょうか？蝙蝠は卵を産まず、ひなに母乳を与えます。ですから、蝙蝠は哺乳類なのです。母乳を子どもに与える生き物はすべて哺乳類です。

（mammal（哺乳類）—ラテン語の mamma が語源、母乳が出る「おっぱい」のこと。）結果として、母乳を与えるすべての動物は、哺乳類、哺乳動物として分類されます。

鳥はみな飛ぶのでしょうか。いいえ。鳥の中には、全く飛べない鳥もいます。駝鳥、エミュー、火食鳥や海に住む鳥にも飛べない鳥がいます。それにしても、駝鳥ほど速く走れる鳥はありません。今は絶滅してしまった、ニュージーランドの鳥であるモアは 17〜20 フィートもの背丈がありました。

鳥の口と蝙蝠の口のちがいは何でしょうか。蝙蝠には歯があります。一方、鳥には歯がなく、口

is shaped like a sword. It is therefore called a BILL, because the ancient word BILL meant a kind of sword. Another word BEAK is also used;— it means a sharp point. Sometimes a beak is called a NIB. The steel pen with which you write is also called a nib.

What do birds make? Birds {build/make} nests,— that is, little dwellings for themselves.

Birds which are hunters,— which live by killing and eating other birds are called BIRDS OF PREY,— just as lions, tigers, and leopards are called BEASTS OF PREY. And their claws are called by the same name as the claws of lions and tigers— TALONS. Eagles, vultures, kites, hawks, falcons, owls:— all have TALONS.

All the leaves of a tree are called FOLIAGE.
Ex.— "The foliage of the maples is red in autumn."

All the feathers on the body of a bird are called the PLUMAGE.
Ex.— "The plumage of the crow is black."

About parts of the body — motion of limbs, &c. Before we talk about the subject I must tell you that in English we do not use the word <u>body</u> in just the same way as in Japanese. We never say "my body", "your body," "his body" in conversation. Generally when we say "body" we mean a DEAD body, a corpse. Instead of saying in English "my is shaped like a sword. It is therefore called a BILL, because the ancient word BILL meant a kind of sword. Another word BEAK is also used; — it means a sharp point. Sometimes a beak is called a NIB. The steel pen with which you write is also called a nib.

What do birds make? Birds {build / make} nests, — that is, little dwellings for themselves.

Birds which are hunters, — which live by killing and eating other birds are called BIRDS OF PREY, — just as lions, tigers and leopards are called BEASTS OF PREY. And their claws are called by the same name as the claws of lions and tigers — TALONS. Eagles, vultures, kites, hawks, falcons, owls: — all have TALONS.

All the leaves of a tree are called FOLIAGE.
Ex. — "The foliage of the maples is red in autumn".

All the feathers on the body of a bird are called the PLUMAGE.
Ex. — "The plumage of the crow is black."

About parts of the body — motion of limbs, &c.

Before we talk about the subject I must tell you that in English we do not use the word <u>body</u> in just the same way as in Japanese. We never say "my body", "your body", "his body" in conversation. Generally when we say "body" we mean a DEAD body, a corpse. Instead of saying in English "my

は剣のような形をしており、BILL（くちばし）と呼ばれています。古代語の BILL は剣の一種を意味していたからです。もうひとつ、BEAK という語も使われます。— BEAK とは、「とがった先っぽ」を意味しています。時に beak は NIB と呼ばれることもあります。よく使うペンや万年筆のペン先もまた、NIB と呼ばれます。

鳥は何をつくりますか？鳥は、巣をつくり（build, make）ます。— すなわち鳥たちの小さな住処を作ります。

狩りをする鳥は — これは他の鳥を殺したり、食べたりする鳥ですが — BIRDS OF PREY（猛禽）と呼ばれます。— ちょうどライオンやトラやヒョウが BEASTS OF PREY（猛獣）と呼ばれるのと同じです。猛禽の爪はライオンやトラの爪と同じように TALONS（鉤爪）と言われます。鷲、禿鷹、鳶、鷹、隼、梟 — すべてこれらの猛禽にはカギヅメがあります。

木の葉全体を、FOLIAGE と言います。
例：— かえでの foliage（葉）は秋に赤く色づきます。

鳥の体に生えている羽全体は、PLUMAGE といいます。
例：— カラスの plumage（羽）は黒い。

体の部位について — 四肢の動きなど

この話題に入る前に触れておかなければならないことは、英語の <u>body</u> という語は日本語の「体」のような使い方をしないということです。my body とか your body、his body とは会話の中で決して言いません。

通常、body という語を使うのは、DEAD body、死体を意味する時です。英語では my body is sick とは言わずに、

body is sick" we would say "I am SICK", &c.

What is the resemblance in the words used for describing a tree and a man? ──── The body of a tree without the branches is called the TRUNK, and so is the body of a man without the legs, arms, and head. Another resemblance is that the branches of a tree are called LIMBS, as our arms and legs are.

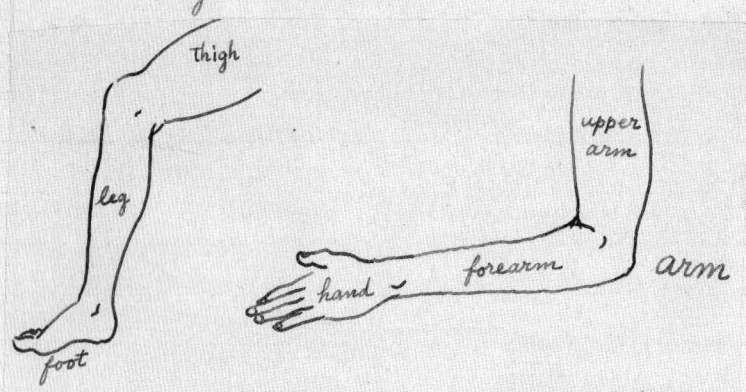

[Diagram of a leg labeled: thigh, leg, foot; and an arm labeled: upper arm, forearm, hand, arm]

The whole of the lower limb except the foot may be called LEG. The whole of the upper limb except the hand may be called ARM. The foot is only what wears the shoe.

[Diagram of a hand labeled: middle finger, index or forefinger, 4th or ring finger, little finger, thumb]

body is sick" we would say "I am SICK", &c.

What is the resemblance in the words used for describing a tree and a man? — The body of a tree without the branches is called the TRUNK, and so is the body of a man without the legs, arms, and head. Another resemblance is that the branches of a tree are called LIMBS, as our arms and legs are.

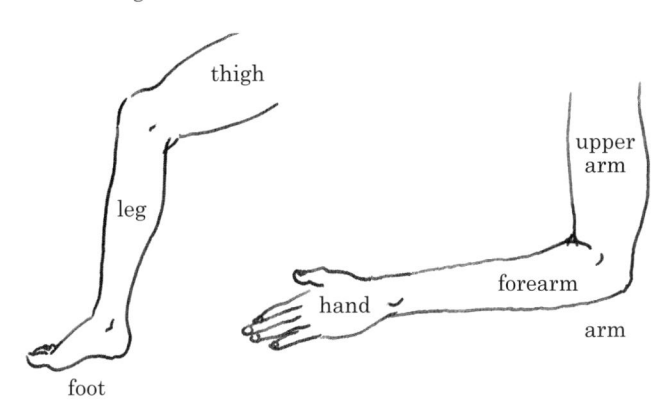

The whole of the lower limb except the foot may be called LEG. The whole of the upper limb except the hand may be called ARM. The foot is only what wears the shoe.

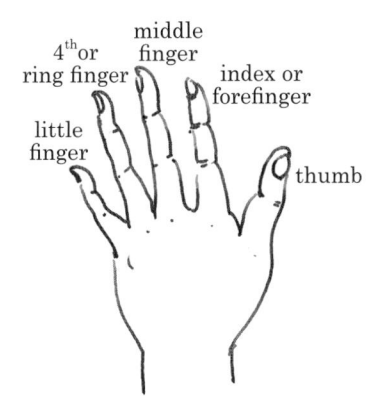

I am SICK. などと表現します。

木と人を表すときの語の類似性とは、どういうものでしょうか？ー枝を切り払った木の本体は TRUNK（幹）と言います。人間の場合、脚、腕、頭を除いた部分も TRUNK（胴体）です。もう一つの類似点は、木の枝は人間の腕や脚と同様に LIMBS と言います。

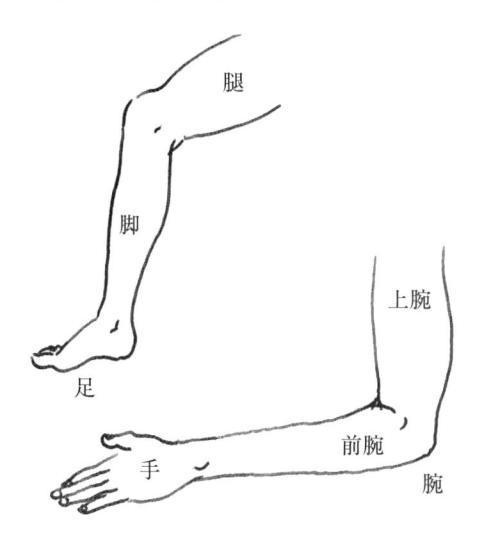

足を除く下肢全体を LEG と言います。手を除いた上肢全体を ARM と言います。FOOT（足）とは靴が履ける部分だけです。

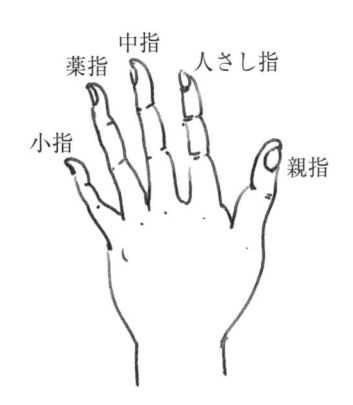

What is the meaning of "fore" in such words as forearm and forefinger? —— It means "before"— just as hindleg means behind-leg.

forelegs   hind legs

Now the forefinger is also called INDEX finger. Index is a word from a Latin word meaning "to show", "to indicate", "to point out". The indexfinger means "the showing finger." By Western nations this finger is used in another curious way. If you see a friend at a distance and want to make him come to you, what do you do? I make a sign: —— "I BECKON to him." But Western people beckon by shaping the indexfinger like a hook (͡) and pulling it toward them.

Can a person express "yes" without speaking? Yes, by a NOD. A "nod" is a very short quick bow of the head only. And when people get sleepy, their heads begin to NOD. So we say of a sleepy child: —— "It is time to go to bed; you are NODDING."

You will often see the word SHRUG in English books. It means to express discontent

What is the meaning of "fore" in such words as forearm and forefinger? – It means "before" – just as hindleg means behind-leg.

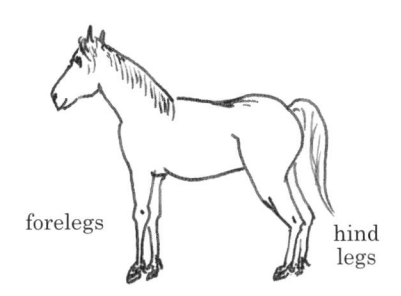

forelegs　hind legs

Now the forefinger is also called INDEX finger. Index is a word from a Latin word meaning "to show", "to indicate", "to point out". The index finger means "the showing finger." By Western nations this finger is used in another curious way. If you see a friend at a distance and want to make him come to you, what do you do? I make a sign：– "I BECKON to him." But Western people beckon by shaping the index finger like a hook (⌒) and pulling it toward them.

Can a person express "yes" without speaking? Yes, by a NOD. A "nod" is a very short quick bow of the head only. And when people get sleepy, their heads begin to NOD. So we say of a sleepy child：–
"It is time to go to bed; you are NODDING."

You will often see the word SHRUG in English books. It means to express discontent

forearm（前腕）や forefinger（人さし指）などの単語に用いられる fore とはどういう意味でしょう？ – fore は before（前）という意味です。hindleg（後肢）が behind leg（後ろの脚）を意味しているのと同様です。

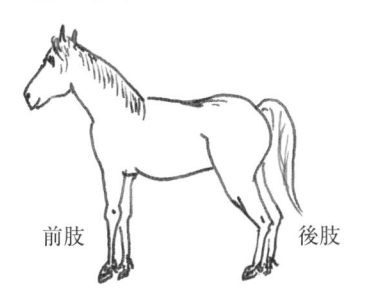

前肢　後肢

ところで forefinger（人さし指）は INDEX finger とも言います。index はラテン語に由来し、「示す」「表す」「指摘する」を意味します。index finger（人さし指）は、the showing finger（指し示す指）という意味です。西洋諸国ではこの指を風変わりな別の方法で用います。遠くに友人がいて、こちらに来てもらいたいときはどうしますか？合図をします。：– I BECKON to him.（彼に向かい手招きします。）西洋人は人さし指を鉤（⌒）のような形に曲げて、先端をクイッと自分のほうに引き寄せます。

yes（「はい」）という意思を、言葉を使わずに伝えることができるでしょうか？できます。うなずくことによって意思を伝えます。nod は頭だけを軽くすばやくこっくりと下げることです。人は眠くなると、こっくりし始めます。それで眠そうな子どもに対しては、次のように言います。
It is time to go to bed; you are NODDING.
（もう寝る時間ですよ。ほら、こっくりしてるでしょう。）
SHRUG（肩をすくめる）という単語を英語の本でよく見かけると思います。
これは、肩を動かすことで

by moving the shoulders. In many other ways Western people move their limbs differently from Orientals. A Japanese carpenter PULLS the saw TO him; a Western carpenter PUSHES it FROM him. Nearly all the powerful movements are made from the shoulder by Western people, so they use a sword very differently. But in writing, drawing, and painting the Chinese or the Japanese are much more skilful, because the movement is quite different. In writing with a pen we write from the WRIST only, but with a Japanese writing-brush the motion is from the ELBOW.

Wrist = the joint on which the hand twists, turns
wrist wrestling

City, Town, Village, Hamlet.

A CITY is a great assemblage of houses. How are the houses arranged? — They are arranged regularly IN streets. What is a street? — A street is a road with houses on both sides.

What is the difference between a CITY and a TOWN? A city is (generally) much larger than a town. Any place with 50,000 inhabitants or more may be called a city. And the largest place in a province may be called a city. Tokyo, Kyoto, Osaka, Kumamoto, by moving the shoulders. In many other ways Western people move their limbs differently from Orientals. A Japanese carpenter PULLS the saw TO him; a Western carpenter PUSHES it FROM him. Nearly all the powerful movements are made from the shoulder by Western people, so they use a sword very differently. But in writing, drawing, and painting the Chinese or the Japanese are much more skillful, because the movement is quite different. In writing with a pen we write from the WRIST only, but with a Japanese writing-brush the motion is from the ELBOW.

Wrist = the joint on which the hand twists, turns.
wrist wrestling.

同意できないことを表します。ほかにもいろいろ、西洋人は東洋人とは違ったやり方で手足を動かします。日本の大工はのこぎりを手前に（TO）引きます（PULLS）が、西洋の大工はのこぎりを手元から（FROM）逆の方向に押します（PUSHES）。西洋人の場合、力仕事のほとんどは肩の動きに関するものであり、そのため刀さばきは東洋とはまったく異なります。ただし、文字を書いたり、デッサンしたり、絵の具で描いたりとなると、中国人や日本人は（西洋人より）はるかに上手です。これは動きがまったく異なるからです。ペンで字を書くとき、手首だけを動かしますが、日本の毛筆の場合、ELBOW（肘）を使って筆を動かします。Wrist（手首）＝手をひねったり、曲げたりする関節。
wrist wrestling.（腕相撲）

City, Town, Village, Hamlet.

都会、町、村、村落

A CITY is a great assemblage of houses. How are the houses arranged? — They are arranged regularly IN streets. What is a street? — A street is a road with houses on both sides.

What is the difference between a CITY and a TOWN? A city is (generally) much larger than a town. Any place with 50,000 inhabitants or more may be called a city. And the largest place in a province may be called a city. Tokyo, Kyoto, Osaka, Kumamoto,

都会は家がたくさん集まったところです。どのような家の並びなのですか？—通り沿いに整然と並んでいます。通りとは何ですか？—通りとは、両側に家が建っている道のことです。
CITY（都会）とTOWN（町）の違いは何ですか？都会は（通常）、町よりもはるかに大きいものです。5万人、あるいはそれ以上の住人がいるところは都会と呼ばれます。そして県や地方で最も大きいところは都会と呼ばれます。東京、京都、大阪、熊本などは都会です。

and so on are cities.

What is the difference between a TOWN and a VILLAGE? What is Dazaifu? It is a village although it is very large. Nearly all the houses are farmers' houses. A village is an agricultural town — a farmers' town. And there is another difference. What is made or manufactured in a village? — Nothing, as a rule. In a village things are bought and sold, — not made. A village is a great agricultural market. But in towns and cities all sorts of things are manufactured — silk, lacquer-ware, porcelain, metal-work, woven-goods, etc.

But there are some towns which have no manufactures, and which are supported only by ships coming and going. What are they called? — PORTS. "Port" means both the harbor and the town; but "harbor" means only the place where the ships rest — not the houses, &c. On the other hand Osaka with all its houses may be called a sea-port. London is also a port.

Port — from Latin, has the meaning of "a gate".

Harbor — from Scandinavian, means "a shelter", "a safe place."

What is a HAMLET? — A very, very small village — even an assembly of three

and so on are cities.

What is the difference between a TOWN and a VILLAGE? What is Dazaifu? It is a village although it is very large. Nearly all the houses are farmers' houses. A village is an agricultural town — a famers' town. And there is another difference. What is made or manufactured in a village? — Nothing, as a rule. In a village things are bought and sold, — not made. A village is a great agricultural market. But in towns and cities all sorts of things are manufactured — silk, lacquer-ware, porcelain, metal-work, woven-goods, etc.

But there are some towns which have no manufactures, and which are supported only by ships coming and going. What are they called? — PORTS. "Port" means both the harbor and the town; but "harbor" means only the place where the ships rest — not the houses, &c. On the other hand Osaka with all its houses may be called a sea-port. London is also a port.

Port — from Latin, has the meaning of "a gate".

Harbor — from Scandinavian, means "a shelter", "a safe place".

What is a HAMLET? — A very, very small village — even an assembly of three

TOWN（町）とVILLAGE（村）の違いは何ですか？太宰府はどうでしょう？規模は大きいが、村です。ほとんどすべての家は、農家です。村とは農業を営む町 — 農民の町のことです。もう１つ別の違いもあります。村では何が作られたり製造されたりしていますか？一般に、何も製造されていません。村では、物が売り買いされてはいますが、製造されているわけではありません。村は、農業の大きな市場なのです。しかし、町や都会では、ありとあらゆるものがつくられています。— 絹や漆器、磁器、金物、織物製品など。

しかし町とは言っても、製造業が何もなく、船の行き来だけでもっているところがあります。そのような町を何と呼びますか？— PORTS（港町）と言います。Portはharbor（港）とtown（町）の両方を含んだ言い方です。しかし、港はただ船が停泊する場所だけのことです。— 家屋などは関係しません。これに対し、家屋がいっぱいある大阪は港湾都市です。ロンドンも同じく、港町です。

Port — ラテン語に由来し、gate（門）という意味です。

Harbor — スカンジナビア語に由来し、shelter（避難所）、safe place（安全な場所）という意味です。

村落 HAMLET とは何ですか？とてもとても小さな村のことです。— 3〜4

or four houses.

City — from the Latin, civitas. This word used to mean a state as well as the chief city, — the place of a state government (Kencho).

Town — from an old English word meaning "a place surrounded by a hedge." In the ancient North there were no stone-walls round a city, — only a ditch and a strong hedge.

<u>Ham</u> was a Danish word for town; and you still see it in such English words as Bucking<u>ham</u>, Notting<u>ham</u>, Birming<u>ham</u>, &c.

Now in order to indicate smallness, we put sometimes LET after a word; say the word is <u>book</u>, then book<u>let</u> is a very small book. So HAMLET is a very small ham or town.

The Latin word <u>villa</u> meant "a farmhouse" — hence our English word "village."

Time

The English system is different from that of other European nations. For example, the French say "12 and a half," which the English never say.

The rule is, mention the minutes, or quarter, or half first — the hour last.

Quarter (Latin, quartus — "4th")

or four houses.

City — from the Latin, civitas. This word used to mean a state as well as the chief city, — the place of a state government (kencho).

Town — from an old English word meaning "a place surrounded by a hedge." In the ancient North there were no stone-walls round a city, — only a ditch and a strong hedge.

<u>Ham</u> was a Danish word for town; and you still see it in such English words as Buckin<u>ham</u>, Nottin<u>ham</u>, Birmin<u>ham</u>, &c.

Now in order to indicate smallness, we put sometimes LET after a word; say the word is <u>book</u>, then book<u>let</u> is a very small book. So HAMLET is a very small ham or town.

The Latin word <u>villa</u> meant "a farmhouse" — hence our English word "village."

Time

The English system is different from that of other European nations. For example, the French say "12 and a half," which the English never say.

The rule is, mention the minutes, or quarter, or half first — the hour last.

Quarter (Latin, quartus — "4th")

軒の家しか集まっていないところを村落と呼びます。

都会 city — ラテン語の civitas に由来します。この語は、かつて主要都市だけでなく、州や県そのものも表していました。— 県庁所在地です。

町 town — 古英語に由来し、生け垣で囲われた場所を意味しています。古代北欧では、市を取り巻く石垣はなく、— 溝と堅固な生け垣のみでした。

<u>Ham</u> はデンマーク語で町 (town) の意味です。今でも Buckin<u>ham</u>（バッキンガム）、Nottin<u>ham</u>（ノッティンガム）、Birmin<u>ham</u>（バーミンガム）といった英語の語彙の中に見られます。

小さいサイズを表す際、私たちは LET を語尾につけることがあります。例えば <u>book</u> の後ろにつけると book<u>let</u> となり、とても小さな本の意味になります。それで、HAMLET はとても小さな村、または町になるわけです。

ラテン語の <u>villa</u> は農家（farmhouse）という意味でした。— ここから英語の village が生まれました。

時間

英国の時間の言い方は、ほかのヨーロッパ諸国の時間の言い方とは異なります。例えばフランス人は 12 時と半分と言いますが、イギリス人は決してそうは言いません。

規則として、まず minutes（分）または quarter（15 分）または half（30 分）を先に言い、最後に hour（時）を言います。

Quarter（ラテン語に由来し、1/4 という意味です。）

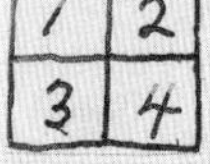
1
2
3
4

The 4th part of anything is called the quarter of it. So 15 minutes is the ¼ of 60 m. or of 1 hour

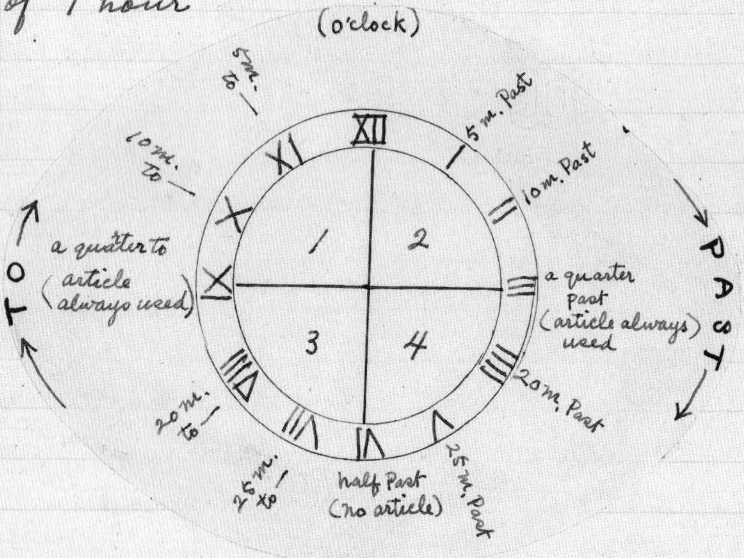
(o'clock)
5 m. to
5 m. Past
10 m. to
10 m. Past
a quarter to (article always used)
a quarter past (article always used)
20 m. to
20 m. Past
25 m. to
25 m. Past
half Past (no article)
TO
PAST
XII
XI
I
II
X
IX
III
VIII
IIII
VII
VI
V
1
2
3
4

Prepositions of Time

General Rules

At — exact time — minutes and hours.
On — days and nights — particular days and nights
In — all inexact time — weeks, months and years.

Examples: —

exact time
We take supper AT 6 o'clock.
When did the students go on the excursion?
We went ON the 6th of last month.

The 4th part of anything is called the quarter of it. So 15 minutes is the 1/4 of 60m. or of 1 hour.

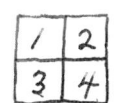

何かの 1/4 の部分はすべて Quarter と言います。15 分は、60 分または 1 時間の 1/4 です。

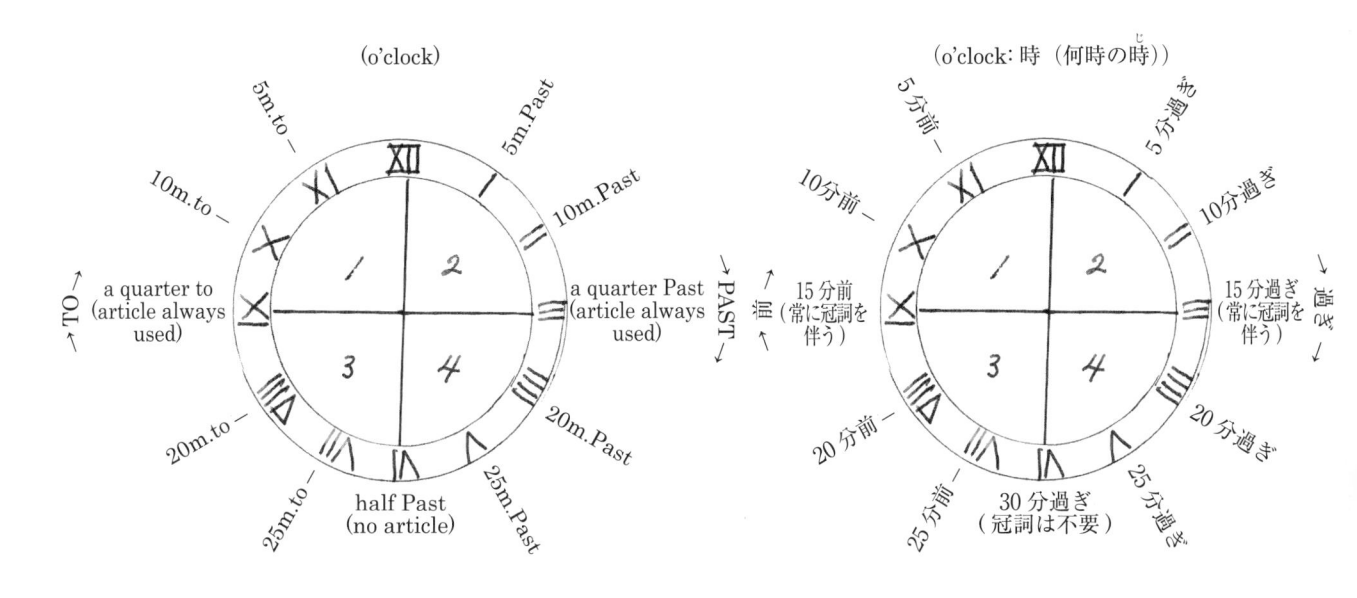

(o'clock)

5m.to — 5m.Past
10m.to — 10m.Past
←TO→ a quarter to (article always used) — a quarter Past (article always used) →PAST→
20m.to — 20m.Past
25m.to — half Past (no article) — 25m.Past

(o'clock: 時（何時の時）)

5分前 — 5分過ぎ
10分前 — 10分過ぎ
←TO→ 15分前（常に冠詞を伴う）— 15分過ぎ（常に冠詞を伴う）→過→
20分前 — 20分過ぎ
25分前 — 30分過ぎ（冠詞は不要）— 25分過ぎ

Prepositions of Time
General Rules

At — exact time — minutes and hours.
On — days and nights — particular days and nights.
In — all inexact time — weeks, months and years.
Examples: —
    We take supper AT (exact time) 6 o'clock.
    When did the students go on the excursion?
    We went ON the 6th of last month.

時の前置詞
一般的ルール

At — 正確な時刻 — 分・時
On — 日と夜 — 特定の日と特定の夜
In — すべての特定できない時間 — 週、月、年
例：—
    六時に（AT）夕食を食べます。（厳密な時刻）
    学生たちはいつ遠足へ行きましたか？
    先月の六日に（ON）行きました。

When was Kumamoto Castle besieged?
In the 10th year of Meiji.

Exceptions:——

Remember ON is used for only particular days or nights —— or parts of particular days and nights :—— ON Tuesday, ON the night of the 10th, ON Saturday morning, &c.

But when "day" only means daytime (time of sunlight) the preposition is IN or BY. When "night" does not mean a particular night, but only night-time (the time of darkness) the preposition is IN or AT. So we say ("by day" or "in the daytime") ("at night" or "in the night")

When do owls fly?—— AT night or IN the night-time. (because no particular night is meant.) When did the old musician come to the Zuihokan and sing for us?—— ON Saturday night. (because a particular night is mentioned.) When do butterflies seek their food?—— BY day, and moths BY night. (because no particular day or night is mentioned.) When did Hideyoshi live?—— ABOUT (uncertain time) three hundred years ago. I think it was ABOUT fifteen or sixteen years ago when a man called Alexander put a barrel of dynamite on a ship, and blew it up.

When was Kumamoto Castle besieged?
In the 10th year of Meiji.

Exceptions:—
　Remember ON is used for only particular days or nights — or parts of particular days and nights:— ON Tuesday, ON the night of the 10th, ON Saturday morning, &c.
　But when "day" only means daytime (time of sunlight) the preposition is IN or BY. When "night" does not mean a particular night, but only night-time (the time of darkness) the preposition is IN or AT. So we say ("by day" or "in the daytime") ("at night" or "in the night")
　When do owls fly? — AT night or IN the night-time. (because no particular night is meant.) When did the old musician come to the Zuihokan and sing for us? — ON Saturday night. (because a particular night is mentioned.) When do butterflies seek their food? — BY day, and moths BY night. (because no particular day or night is mentioned.) When did Hideyoshi live? — ABOUT (uncertain time) three hundred years ago. I think it was ABOUT fifteen or sixteen years ago when a man called Alexander put a barrel of dynamite on a ship, and blew it up.

熊本城はいつ包囲されましたか？
明治十年に（IN）です。

例外：—
On は特定の日や特定の夜—または特定の日や特定の夜の一部に使われることを忘れないでください。：— ON Tuesday（火曜日に）、ON the night of the 10th（10日の夜に）、ON Saturday morning（土曜日の朝に）など。
ただし、day が日中（日が出ている時間）を表す場合、前置詞は IN または BY になります。night が特定の夜を表さず、夜の時間帯しか表さない場合は、前置詞が IN または AT になります。そのため、by day（日中）または in the daytime（日中）、at night（夜に）または in the night（夜間に）と表記するのです。
フクロウはいつ飛びますか？— AT night（夜に）または IN the night-time（夜間に）飛びます（特定の日の夜が示されているのではないゆえに。）いつその老音楽家が瑞邦館にやって来て、歌を歌ってくれたのですか？— 土曜日の晩（ON）です（特定の日の晩が示されている）。
蝶はいつ食べ物を探しに出ますか？— 日中（BY）です。蛾は夜に（BY）食べ物を探しに出ます（特定の日の昼または夜が示されていない）。秀吉はいつごろ生きた人ですか？— およそ（ABOUT）三百年前です（不確かな時間）。アレクサンダーという男がダイナマイトがつまった樽を船に積んでこれを爆破したのは、たしか15〜16年前のことだったと思います。

Englishman wore swords IN the eighteenth century.

I came AT 5 minutes to 12 o'clock, and asked to see my friend. I was told I could see him IN half-an-hour. I will see him IN a minute. I will see him AT 1 minute past 12 o'clock.

Earthquakes!

Did you feel the earthquake the other day? (the other day — idiom = a few days ago; the other night = a few nights ago; the other week = several weeks ago)

Yes, I felt the earthquake last week. Was it a strong shock or a weak one? It was a weak one, and lasted about two minutes. (Note that the word SHOCK means a SHAKE —— one moment only.) Were you in the college when the shock TOOK PLACE (or happened)?

A storm
An earthquake } TAKES PLACE
A quarrel
A meeting

Englishman wore swords IN the eighteenth century.

I came AT 5 minutes to 12 o'clock, and asked to see my friend. I was told I could see him IN half-an-hour. I will see him IN a minute. I will see him AT 1 minute past 12 o'clock.

Earthquakes!

Did you feel the earthquake the other day? (the other day — idiom = a few days ago; the other night = a few nights ago; the other week = several weeks ago)

Yes, I felt the earthquake last week. Was it a strong shock or a weak one? It was a weak one, and lasted about two minutes. (Note that the word SHOCK means a SHAKE — one moment only.) Were you in the college when the shock TOOK PLACE (or happened)?

A storm	
An earthquake	TAKES PLACE
A quarrel	
A meeting	

18世紀には（IN）、イギリス人は剣を身につけていました。

私は12時5分前に（AT）来て、友だちに会わせてもらうように頼みました。30分後に（IN）会えると言われました。彼とはすぐに（IN a minute）会えることでしょう。私は12時1分に（AT）彼と会います。

地震だ！

先日は地震を感じましたか？（the other day — 慣用句＝2〜3日前；the other night＝2〜3日前の晩；the other week＝数週間前）

はい、先週、私は地震を感じました。強い揺れでしたか、それとも弱い揺れでしたか？弱い揺れで、2分ほど続きました。
（SHOCK（衝撃）という単語は一瞬のSHAKE（揺れ）という意味。）揺れが起きた（TOOK PLACE）とき、あなたは学校にいましたか？

嵐	
地震	TAKES PLACE
口げんか	（発生する／おこる／行われる）
ミーティング	

Yes, I was indoors, and I was STARTLED (or afraid) for a moment.

Difference between "startled" and "afraid":— "startled" means "very suddenly afraid because of surprise."

Did the house tremble (or shake)?

Shake
Tremble } of persons or things

What kind of noise was it? ——— I did not hear the noise because I was { sound asleep that morning. (or fast asleep)

These two idioms are always used.

Sound (adj.) = healthy, strong (not the word meaning "noise").

(1.) Sound = noise (noun)
(2) Sound = strong, healthy, solid (adj.)
(1) Fast = swift, rapid (adj.)
(2) Fast = tight, well-closed, like a box difficult to open.

"I cannot open the box ——— it is fast."

Fast asleep ——— the mind is like something hard to open.

What kind of noise does a wooden house make during an earthquake? ——— It makes a noise like the sound of wood breaking ——— a creaking noise, but sometimes worse.

Was the shock felt <u>anywhere else</u>? (idiom, this is the better idiom.)

Yes, I was indoors, and I was STARTLED for a moment.　　　　　　　　　or afraid

Difference between "startled" and "afraid":— "startled" means "very suddenly afraid because of surprise."

Did the house tremble (or shake)?

Shake　　⎫
Tremble　⎭ of persons or things

What kind of noise was it? — I did not hear the noise because I was ⎧ sound asleep that morning.
⎨ or
⎩ fast asleep

These two idioms are always used.

Sound (adj.) = healthy, strong (not the word meaning "noise").

(1) Sound = noise (noun)
(2) Sound = strong, healthy, solid (adj.)
(1) Fast = swift, rapid (adj.)
(2) Fast = tight, well-closed, like a box difficult to open.

"I cannot open the box — it is fast."

Fast asleep. — the mind is like something hard to open.

What kind of noise does a wooden house make during an earthquake? — It makes a noise like the sound of wood breaking – a creaking noise, but sometimes worse.

Was the shock felt <u>anywhere else</u>? (idiom, this is the better idiom.)

はい、そのとき私は室内にいて、一瞬ハッとビックリしました（怖くなりました。）

startled と afraid のちがい：— startled は「びっくりした故に突然とても怖くなること」を表す。

家は震え（または揺れ）ましたか？

Shake（揺れる）⎫
Tremble（震える）⎭ 人または物が

どんな音でしたか？—その朝はよく寝ていたので（寝入っていたので）聞こえませんでした。

これら2つの慣用句は頻繁に用いられます。

Sound（形容詞）＝健康的、強い（音を意味する単語ではない。）

(1)Sound＝音（名詞）
(2)Sound＝強い、健康的、しっかりした（形容詞）
(1)Fast＝素早い、急な（形容詞）
(2)Fast＝開けにくい箱のようにしっかりと、よく閉まっている

「箱を開けることができない—フタがしっかり閉まっています。」

Fast asleep（ぐっすり寝入る）—心とは何か開け難いもののようだ。

地震のとき、木造住宅はどんな音を立てますか？—木が割れるような音—（ミシミシという音）が出ますが、ときにはもっとひどいことがあります。

<u>どこかほかの場所</u>でも揺れは感じられましたか？（慣用句はこちらの方がよい。）

(any¹where ²else?)
(in¹ any² other³ p⁴lace?)
Yes, AT Kagoshima, AT Saga, ——.

Uses of "straw" —— The word "straw" is collective; and when it means material it has NO ARTICLE. If you say "straws", that means 2 or 3 stalks.
Tree — trunk; bamboo and plant —— stem; grass and grain —— stalk.

What is straw? —— "Straw" is the name given to the stalks of rice, wheat, rye, oats, barley, &c. after they are cut. (rice-straw, oat-straw, wheat-straw, &c.)

Straw is used for covering the roofs of houses. What is that kind of a roof called? —— It is called a thatched roof, and "to thatch" a roof means "to cover it with straw." In hot countries we have "cane-thatch"; "bamboo-thatch" and "palm-thatch".

Straw is also used { to feed / for the food of } horses and cattle. (cows, bulls, calves, oxen, &c.) Straw is used to make ropes and cords. (Ropes and cords are made out of straw.) Straw is also used for making many kinds of paper. (Note the word "paper". It is a material noun, and has no plural. "Papers" do not mean pieces of paper only, but documents.)

$\begin{Bmatrix} 1 \quad 2 \\ \text{anywhere else?} \\ 1 \quad 2 \quad 3 \quad 4 \\ \text{in any other place?} \end{Bmatrix}$

Yes, AT Kagoshima, AT Saga, ….

Uses of "straw" — The word "straw" is collective; and when it means material it has NO ARTICLE. If you say "straw<u>s</u>", that means 2 or 3 stalks.

Tree — trunk; bamboo and plant — stem; grass and grain — stalk.

What is straw? — "Straw" is the name given to the stalks of rice, wheat, rye, oats, barley, &c. after they are cut. (rice-straw, oat-straw, wheat-straw, &c.)

Straw is used for covering the roofs of houses. What is that kind of a roof called? — It is called a thatched roof, and "to thatch" a roof means "to cover it with straw." In hot countries we have "cane-thatch", "bamboo-thatch" and "palm-thatch".

Straw is also used $\begin{Bmatrix} \text{to feed} \\ \text{for the food of} \end{Bmatrix}$ horses and cattle. (cows, bulls, calves, oxen, &c.) Straw is used to make ropes and cords. (Ropes and cords are made out of straw.) Straw is also used for making many kinds of paper. (Note the word "paper". It is a material noun, and has no plural. "Papers" do not mean pieces of paper only, but documents.)

$\begin{Bmatrix} 1 \quad 2 \\ \text{Anywhere else?} \\ （場所　どこかほかの） \\ 1 \quad 2 \quad 3 \quad 4 \\ \text{In any other place?} \\ （〜において、どこか　ほかの　場所？） \end{Bmatrix}$

はい、鹿児島で、佐賀で…。

straw の使い方 — straw（「藁」）は集合名詞的に使われ、物質名詞のときは冠詞がつきません。straws と複数形になると、2〜3本の藁束の意味になります。

樹木 — trunk（幹）、
竹および植物 — stem（幹あるいは茎）、
草および穀類 — stalk（茎）

藁とは何ですか？ — 藁とは稲や麦、ライ麦、烏麦、大麦などが刈り取られた後の茎の総称です（米の藁、烏麦の藁、麦藁など）

藁は家屋の屋根を葺くために用いられます。そうした屋根を何と呼びますか？ — 藁葺き屋根と言います。to thatch a roof（屋根に藁を葺く）は、to cover it with straw（藁で覆う）という意味です。暑い国では、砂糖黍や竹、椰子で屋根を葺くことがあります。

藁は、馬や家畜（雌牛、去勢していない雄牛、子牛、雄牛など）の餌に（あるいは食物に）使います。藁はロープや縄を編むのにも使われます（ロープと縄は藁でできています）。藁は多くの種類の紙をつくるのにも用いられます。（paper という語に注意。物質名詞であり複数形はない。Papers は1枚1枚の紙を意味しません。書類／文書といった意味になります。）

1. — paper — no plural — the substance on which we write.
2. — papers — public or private documents. (a lawyer's papers.)
3. — papers — (in commerce only) different kinds of paper.
4. — papers — newspapers.

Straw is also used for floor-mats (<u>tatami</u>) and for <u>zori</u> and <u>waraji</u> which are different kinds of sandals. To make mats and so on the straw is WOVEN. What other things are woven besides straw? Silk, cotton, flax, and wool. What makes silk? — Silk is made by silkworms, — a kind of caterpillar.

What is cotton? — Cotton grows on a plant in pads. Wool is the name given to the curly hair that grows on the bodies of sheep and some kinds of goats. Fur is the name given to the short, fine hair on such animals as cats, rabbits, seals, foxes, and tigers. Animals like dogs, horses, camels, wolves, bears, and cattle — which have coarse hair — have not FUR.

Straw is also used to make hats and the sails of fishing-boats. A hat has a brim; a cap has only a peak, and sometimes not even that.

1. – paper – no plural – the substance on which we write.
2. – papers – public or private documents. (a lawyer's papers.)
3. – papers – (in commerce only) different kinds of paper.
4. – papers – newspapers.

Straw is also used for floor-mats (tatami) and for zori and waraji which are different kinds of sandals. To make mats and so on the straw is WOVEN. What other things are woven besides straw? Silk, cotton, flax, and wool. What makes silk? – Silk is made by silkworms, – a kind of caterpillar.

What is cotton? – Cotton grows on a plant in pads.* Wool is the name given to the curly hair that grows on the bodies of sheep and some kinds of goats. Fur is the name given to the short, fine hair on such animals as cats, rabbits, seals, foxes, and tigers. Animals like dogs, horses, camels, wolves, bears, and cattle – which have coarse hair – have not FUR.

Straw is also used to make hats and the sails of fishing-boats. A hat has a brim; a cap has only a peak, and sometimes not even that.

1. paper － 複数形なし－その上に筆記するもの
2. papers － 公的または私的文書（弁護士の文書）
3. papers －（商業用のみ）異なるタイプの紙
4. papers － 新聞

藁はマット（畳）や草履、草鞋（それぞれサンダルの種類）にも使われます。畳などをつくる場合、藁を編みます（WOVEN）。藁のほかにも、何が編まれますか？ 絹、綿、亜麻、毛糸です。絹は何からできていますか？ －絹は蚕（かいこ）から取れるものです。－蚕は一種の毛虫です。

綿とは何ですか？－綿はさやの中で育ちます。wool（羊毛）は羊やある種の山羊の体に生える巻き毛の名前です。fur（毛皮）は猫や兎、海豹（あざらし）、狐、虎などの短く細い体毛の名前です。犬や馬、駱駝、狼、熊、牛など、ザラザラした体毛を持つ動物の毛皮には fur はありません。

藁は帽子や漁船の帆をつくるのにも用いられます。帽子（hat）にはツバがあり、キャップ帽にはひさしがついていますが、ついていないものもあります。

hat   cap

* ノートには Cotton grows on a plant in pads. とありそのまま復元してあるが、これはおそらく筆記の際の誤記で、正しくは Cotton grows on a plant in pods. であろう。

The Sky

Azure = the blue of the sky

What does the sky look like? —— It looks like a great blue arch or vault bending over the world.

Arch —— from Latin *arcus*, a bow (*yumi*).

Vault —— from Old French *vaulter*, to bend, to curve.

"For the blue sky ·BENDS over all." —
                                            Coleridge.

To vault = to jump over a thing with the help of the hands.

A roof or ceiling which is curved or bent like a bow is called a VAULT.

```
                Arabian word — means "overhead"
                    zenith
                  ╱────────╲
                 ╱          ╲
                ╱            ╲
        Greek horos — end, limit, boundary.
           zone — a belt, girdle, obi.
    horizon                      horizon
         the obi, or girdle of the world's end.
```

Is the blue or azure of the sky the same all over?

No, the color is deepest at the zenith and grows PALE toward the horizon.

What parts of the horizon are most beautiful, and when?

The Sky

Azure = the blue of the sky

What does the sky look like? — It looks like a great blue arch or vault bending over the world.

Arch — from Latin <u>arcus</u>, a bow (<u>yumi</u>).

Vault — from Old French <u>vaulter</u>, to bend, to curve.

"For the blue sky BENDS over all."—
                                Coleridge.

To vault = to jump over a thing with the help of the hands.

A roof or ceiling which is curved or bent like a bow is called a VAULT.

```
                Arabian word — means "overhead"
                        Zenith

             Greek horos — end, limit, boundary.
             Zone — a belt, girdle, obi.
   horizon                                    horizon
          the obi, or girdle of the world's end.
```

Is the blue or azure of the sky the same all over?

No, the color is deepest at the zenith and grows PALE toward the horizon.

What parts of the horizon are most beautiful, and when?

空

Azure（空色）＝空の青さ

空はどう見えますか？ー空は地球にかかった大きな真っ青なアーチ、または天蓋のように見えます。

Arch — ラテン語の <u>arcus</u> に由来し、bow（弓）の意味。

Vault — 古フランス語の <u>vaulter</u> に由来し、to bend（曲げる）、to curve（湾曲させる）の意味。

For the blue sky BENDS over all.（青空が万物の上に身を屈めているから）ーコールリッジ

To vault ＝両手を使って、ものを飛び越えること。

弓のように曲がった屋根や天井はVAULT（アーチ型天井）と呼ばれます。

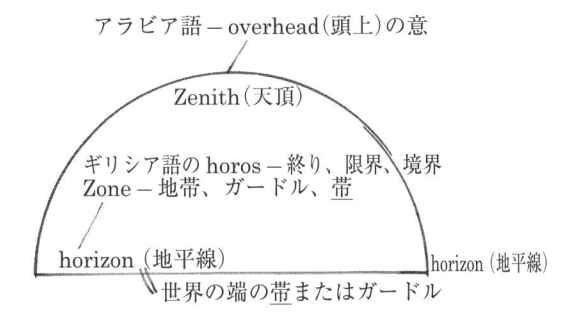

```
              アラビア語 — overhead（頭上）の意
                      Zenith（天頂）

           ギリシア語の horos — 終り、限界、境界
           Zone — 地帯、ガードル、帯
   horizon（地平線）                        horizon（地平線）
          世界の端の帯またはガードル
```

空の青さもしくは蒼さは、どこでも同じですか？

いいえ、天頂では青が一番深く、地平線に向かっていくにつれて PALE（青白い）になります。地平線のどの部分が一番美しいですか？また、いつ美しくなりますか？

The west and east, at sunset and sunrise.

At sunrise the eastern sky is sometimes all red or crimson; and at sunset the western horizon is often a beautiful yellow or golden color, and sometimes orange, and sometimes vermilion, or even blood-red.

Why can we not always see the azure? Because it is often covered by clouds,— white, black, grey, and all colors.

What are the shapes of clouds? Can they be counted?   No,— not exactly. The shapes of clouds are innumerable and countless, and every cloud is constantly changing its shape; and no two clouds have ever had exactly the same shape since the beginning of the world. But scientific men divide clouds into four principal classes.

Does the sky look the same in all countries? Not quite. As we go south towards the equator, the sky seems to sink lower and to become more and more blue. In Japan it looks very high.

At night the sky is full of stars; but in all countries the stars are not the same. On a clear night we see also stretching across the sky a white band like a river, and some have called it the River of Heaven. But the English name is the Milky Way.

The west and east, at sunset and sunrise.

At sunrise the eastern sky is sometimes all red or crimson; and at sunset the western horizon is often a beautiful yellow or golden color, and sometimes orange, and sometimes vermilion, or even blood-red.

Why can we not always see the azure? Because it is often covered by clouds,— white, black, grey, and all colors.

What are the shapes of clouds? Can they be counted? No, — not exactly. The shapes of clouds are innumerable and countless, and every cloud is constantly changing its shape; and no two clouds have ever had exactly the same shape since the beginning of the world. But scientific men divide clouds into four principal classes.

Does the sky look the same in all countries? Not quite. As we go south towards the equator, the sky seems to sink lower and to become more and more blue. In Japan it looks very high.

At night the sky is full of stars; but in all countries the stars are not the same. On a clear night we see also stretching across the sky a white band like a river, and some have called it the River of Heaven. But the English name is the Milky Way.

西と東、日の入りと日の出のときが一番美しくなります。日の出のとき、東の空が真赤または深紅に染まり、日の入りのとき西の地平線が美しい黄色または金色、ときにはオレンジや朱色、血のような赤になります。

どうして、いつも青い空を見ることができないのですか？ 白や黒、灰色など、ありとあらゆる色の雲に覆われてしまうことがあるからです。

雲はどんな形をしていますか？ 雲は数えられますか？いいえ、— 正確には数えられません。雲の形は無数にあり、どの雲も常に形を変えています。この世の初まり以来、どの雲も同じ形になったことがありません。しかし科学者は雲を4つの主要なものに分類しています。

空は、世界中どの国でも同じように見えますか？必ずしもそうではありません。赤道に向かって南下するに従い、空が低くなり、青さも増してきます。日本では空はとても高く見えます。

夜になると、空は星でいっぱいになります。しかし、見える星はすべての国で同じというわけではありません。晴れた夜には、川のような白い帯が空にかかって延びているのを見ることができますが、ある人たちはそれを天の川と呼んでいます。英語では the Milky Way と言います。

This name was given by the old Greeks. They said that the mother of God, or nurse (uba) let her milk fall while carrying the child across the sky. Another name for the sky is the heaven(s). But we must always say THE heaven(s), for the world "heaven" by itself means "gokuraku". If spelled with a big "H", it means God, Providence, &c.

1. Heaven = Providence, the Supreme, etc.
2. the heaven = the sky
   the heavens = the sky } Both forms are used.
3. heaven = <u>gokuraku</u>, paradise, the world of happiness after death.

Preliminary Exercises on Prepositions

At —— seconds, minutes, hours —— exact time.
On —— days and nights
In —— weeks, months —— all big time.

When do you take breakfast, dinner, and supper? We take breakfast AT 6 o'clock in the morning, dinner AT noon (or 12 o'clock or midday), and supper AT 8 o'clock. ⎯ exact time

Do you study every day IN the year? No; we have a half-holiday ON Saturdays and no classes ON Sundays. ⎯ particular days — on

This name was given by the old Greeks. They said that the mother of God, or nurse (uba) let her milk fall while carrying the child across the sky. Another name for the sky is the heaven(s). But we must always say THE heaven(s), for the word* "heaven" by itself means "gokuraku". If spelled with a big "H", it means God, Providence, &c.

1. Heaven = Providence, the Supreme, etc.
2. the heaven = the sky
   the heavens = the sky } Both forms are used.
3. heaven = gokuraku, paradise, the world of happiness after death.

Preliminary Exercises on Prepositions

At – seconds, minutes, hours – exact time.
On – days and nights
In – weeks, months – all big time.

When do you take breakfast, dinner, and supper? We take breakfast AT 6 o'clock in the morning, dinner AT noon (or 12 o'clock or midday), and supper AT 8 o'clock. (exact time)

Do you study every day IN the year? No; we have a half-holiday ON Saturdays and no classes ON Sundays. (particular days – on)

* ノートには world となっているが、word の誤記と考え訂正した。

この呼び名をつけたのは古代ギリシャ人でした。神の母、または乳母（nurse）が、子どもを抱えて空を渡っていくとき、乳をこぼしてしまったと言われています。空につけられたもう1つの名称は heaven(s)（天）です。これを言う場合、常に THE heaven(s) としなければなりません。なぜなら、heaven（天国）それ自体は「極楽」という意味だからです。大文字の H で綴る場合、神や摂理（神意）などを意味します。

1. Heaven = 摂理、神など
2. the heaven = the sky
   the heavens = the sky } 両形式が使われる。
3. heaven = 極楽、楽園、死後の幸福な世界

前置詞の予備練習

At －秒、分、時－正確な時刻
On －日と夜
In －週、月－大きな時の単位

いつ朝食、昼食、夕食を食べますか？朝食は朝6時に（AT）、昼食は正午（12時（丁度）または真昼）に（AT）、夕食は午後8時に（AT）食べます。

あなたは1年中毎日学校へ行っていますか？（または勉強していますか？）いいえ、土曜日（On－特定の日）は半日、日曜日（On）は終日休みです。

When did Saigo Takamori besiege Kumamoto Castle?

IN the 10th year of Meiji. (all large)

Sunday means the Day of the Sun, because the ancient people of the North worshipped on that day.

Monday — the Day of the Moon — for the same reason.

Tuesday — Tyr's dæg, or Tyr's day. Who was Tyr? The old Northern God of courage. There was once an aweful wolf (ōkami) whose mouth opened from earth to heaven. And the gods were afraid and wanted to tie the wolf. But the wolf suspected this and said, "If I let you tie me, one of you must first put his hand into my mouth." Then all the gods were afraid except Tyr. Tyr put his hand in the wolf's mouth. Then the wolf let the gods tie him. But when he found the gods had tied him fast, he bit off Tyr's hand.

Wednesday — the Day of Woden, or Odin — father of all the Northern gods. Our word "god" is supposed to come from his name.

Thursday — Thor's Day. Thor was the God of strength, the God of Battle, the fighting God. He fought with a hammer. Thunder was said to be the sound of his hammer.

Friday — the Day of Frigga, wife of Odin.

When did Saigo Takamori besiege Kumamoto Castle? (all large)

IN the 10th year of Meiji.

Sunday means the Day of the Sun, because the ancient people of the North worshipped on that day.

Monday – the Day of the Moon – for the same reason.

Tuesday – Tyr's day, or Tyr's day. Who was Tyr? The old Northern God of courage. There was once an awful* wolf (okami) whose mouth opened from earth to heaven. And the gods were afraid and wanted to tie the wolf. But the wolf suspected this and said, "If I let you tie me, one of you must first put his hand into my mouth." Then all the gods were afraid except Tyr. Tyr put his hand in the wolf's mouth. Then the wolf let the gods tie him. But when he found the gods had tied him fast, he bit off Tyr's hand.

Wednesday – the Day of Woden, or Odin – father of all the Northern gods. Our word "god" is supposed to come from his name.

Thursday – Thor's Day, Thor was the God of strength, the God of Battle, the fighting God. He fought with a hammer. Thunder was said to be the sound of his hammer.

Friday – the Day of Frigga, wife of Odin.

* ノートには aweful となっているが、awful の誤記と考え訂正した。

西郷隆盛が熊本城（大文字で表記する）を包囲したのはいつですか？
明治10年です。
Sunday とは、太陽の日という意味です。これは、古代の北欧の人がその日に太陽を礼拝していたからです。
Monday－月の日－上記と同じ理由

Tuesday－Tyr（ティール）の日（Tyr's day）。Tyrとは誰か？古代スカンジナビアの勇気の神。昔、天地に届くほど大きく口を開けた恐ろしい狼がいました。神々は恐れ、狼を縛り付けたいと思っていました。しかし、狼はそのことを知り、こう言いました。「私を縛りたいのであれば、その前にお前たちのうち誰か1人が私の口の中に手を入れろ。」これを聞いて、Tyr を除く神全員が恐れおののきました。Tyr は狼の口に手を入れました。すると狼は甘んじて神々に自分を縛らせました。しかし、神々が狼をしっかりと縛り付けるやいなや、狼は Tyr の手を噛みちぎってしまったのです。

Wednesday－Woden（ウォーデン）またはOdin（オーディン）の日。北欧神話のすべての神々の父。英語の god も彼の名前から来ていると考えられています。
Thursday－Thor（トール）の日。Thor は力の神、戦闘の神であり、戦う神です。槌を武器にして戦いました。Thunder（雷）は、彼が槌を振るう時の音だと言われています。
Friday－Frigga（Odin の妻）の日。

Saturday —— This is the only day not named by the Northmen. It was named by the Romans. It means Saturn's Day. Who was Saturn? The Roman God of Time.

What does "month" mean? One month = the time of one moon.

I had a letter from my father last week. He asked me to visit him this month. But I could not go until next month. It would be easier to go IN June or IN July.

The rule :——

Before NEXT, LAST, TOMORROW, TODAY, YESTERDAY no prepositions.

When do you find time to amuse yourselves? ON Sundays we have time to amuse ourselves.

How did you spend last Sunday? We had a game of baseball last Sunday. We played at baseball last Sunday. (no preposition)

To take { breakfast, dinner, etc.
fresh air at ——
a swim in ——
a ride
a boat
a train for ——
a lesson in ——
pleasure in ——

Saturday — This is the only day not named by the Northmen. It was named by the Romans. It means Saturn's Day. Who was Saturn? The Roman God of Time.

What does "month" mean? One month = the time of one moon.

I had a letter from my father last week. He asked me to visit him this month. But I could not go until next month. It would be easier to go IN June or IN July.
The rule :—

Before NEXT, LAST, TOMORROW, TODAY, YESTERDAY no prepositions.

When do you find time to amuse yourselves? ON Sundays we have time to amuse ourselves.

How did you spend last Sunday?
We had a game of baseball last Sunday.
We played at baseball last Sunday. (no prepositions.)

To take ⎰ breakfast, dinner, etc.
　　　　 fresh air at ___
　　　　 a swim in ___
　　　　 a ride
　　　　 a boat
　　　　 a train for ___
　　　　 a lesson in ___
　　　　 pleasure in ___

Saturday — これだけが唯一、北欧人によって付けられていない語です。ローマ人によって付けられました。Saturn（サトゥルヌス）の日という意味です。Saturnとは誰か？ Saturnとはローマの時間の神です。

month（月）の意味は何ですか？ ひと月 ＝ 月が満ち欠けする時間。

先週、父から手紙を受け取りました。今月、来るようにとのことでした。しかし、来月まで彼のもとへ行くことができません。6月か7月（IN）のほうがもっと行きやすいのですが。

ルール

NEXT、LAST、TOMORROW、TODAY、YESTERDAYの前に前置詞は置きません。

自分で楽しめる時間はいつですか？
日曜日には遊べる時間があります。

先週の日曜日は何をしましたか？先週の日曜日は、野球の試合をしました。先週の日曜日は野球をしました。（前置詞なし）

To take ⎰ breakfast, dinner, etc.（食事をとる）
　　　　 fresh air at ___（で新鮮な空気を吸う）
　　　　 a swim in ___（で泳ぐ）
　　　　 a ride（乗物に乗る）
　　　　 a boat（船に乗る）
　　　　 a train for ___（行きの列車に乗る）
　　　　 a lesson in ___（のレッスンを受ける）
　　　　 pleasure in ___（を楽しむ）

Prepositions of Places

<u>In</u> — all enclosed spaces, whether by 2 or 3 or 4 sides, are expressed with the help of IN.

<u>On</u> — surface — whether up, down, or perpendicular.

<u>At</u> — exact place.

Where do the clouds form? — IN the sky. We always say "IN the sky". Why? Because the sky seems to be an enclosed space. ⌒(in)

Where are the students of Class P.III.B.? They are now IN Room No. 13.

What are they doing now? — They are sitting ON their chairs AT their desks. ("at" gives the exact place of the chairs or stools.)

What else are they doing? — They are writing ON sheets of paper and IN note-books. (A sheet of paper is not enclosed: it is all surface. But a book is a thing enclosed by 2 sides and a back.)

What has the teacher been doing? — He has been writing with chalk ON the board. (Whether the surface is down or up makes no difference.) There is a fly ON the ceiling. There is a picture ON the wall. There is a book ON the floor.

Where is the school bell hung? — The

Prepositions of Places

In — all enclosed spaces, whether by 2 or 3 or 4 sides, are expressed with the help of IN.

On — surface — whether up, down, or perpendicular.

At — exact place.

Where do the clouds form? — IN the sky. We always say "IN the sky." Why? Because the sky seems to be an enclosed space.

Where are the students of class P.Ⅲ.B.? They are now IN Room No.13.

What are they doing now? — They are sitting ON their chairs AT their desks. ("at" gives the exact place of the chairs or stools.)

What else are they doing? — They are writing ON sheets of paper and IN note-books. (A sheet of paper is not enclosed: it is all surface. But a book is a thing enclosed by 2 sides and a back.)

What has the teacher been doing? — He has been writing with chalk ON the board. (Whether the surface is down or up makes no difference.) There is a fly ON the ceiling. There is a picture ON the wall. There is a book ON the floor.

Where is the school bell hung? — The

場所の前置詞

In－2面、3面、4面に囲まれた、すべての閉じられた空間は IN を用いて表します。

On－表面－上または下、垂直でも

At－正確な場所

雲はどこで生まれるのですか？－空（IN）です。英語では常に IN the sky と言います。なぜですか？空は閉じられた空間と考えられているためです。

P.Ⅲ.B*の学生はどこにいますか？
彼らは今、13号室に（IN）います。
彼らは今、何をしているのですか？－彼らは椅子に（ON）座り、机に（AT）向かっています。（at は椅子または腰掛けの正確な場所を示している。）
そのほかには何をしているのですか？－紙や（ON）ノートに（IN）書いています。（紙一枚一枚は閉じられておらず、すべて面です。しかし本は二面と背表紙で閉じられています。）
先生は何をしていましたか？－彼はチョークで黒板に（ON）文字を書いていました。（面の上下は関係がない。）天井に（ON）蠅がいます。壁に（ON）絵がかかっています。床に（ON）本が置かれています。
学校の鐘はどこにつり下げられていますか？

* 予科三級乙をこのように英語で呼んだ。

school bell is hung AT the door of the building where the teachers' room is.

Where is Mr. Akizuki's picture hung? —— IN the Zuihokwan ON the wall. Where does Mr. B live? (Give an imaginary address.) —— He lives AT No. 3, IN Tsuboi, IN Kumamoto.
He is now <u>at</u> school.
   <u>in</u> Kumamoto.
   <u>in</u> Kumamoto Ken.
   <u>in</u> Kyushu.
   <u>in</u> Japan.
   <u>in</u> the Orient.

Where do fishes live? —— and where do birds sing? —— Fishes live IN the water, birds sing IN the trees. (Why? —— Because the bird is surrounded or enclosed by leaves, just as fish are surrounded by water.) But if you see the bird, you can say "It is ON the branches, &c. When we see a <u>semi</u>, we say "There is a <u>semi</u> ON that tree." But when we only hear it and cannot see it, we say "IN the tree". Crickets sing IN the grass. The grass hides them, encloses them, surrounds them.

But there are queer exceptions: ——
When you look IN a looking-glass what do

school bell is hung AT the door of the building where the teachers' room is.

Where is Mr. Akizuki's picture hung? — IN the Zuihokwan ON the wall. Where does Mr. B live? (Give an imaginary address.) — He lives AT NO.3, IN Tsuboi, IN Kumamoto.

He is now at school.
    in Kumamoto.
    in Kumamoto Ken.
    in Kyusyu.
    in Japan.
    in the Orient.

Where do fishes live? — and where do birds sing? — Fishes live IN the water, birds sing IN the trees. (Why? — Because the bird is surrounded or enclosed by leaves, just as fish are surrounded by water.) But if you see the bird, you can say "It is ON the branches, &c. When we see a semi, we say "There is a semi ON that tree." But when we only hear it and cannot see it, we say "IN the tree". Crickets sing IN the grass. The grass hides them, encloses them, surrounds them.

But there are queer exceptions:—
When you look IN a looking-glass what do

— 職員室のある建物のドアのところに（AT）つり下げられています。
秋月先生の絵はどこに飾られていますか？ — 瑞邦館の壁に（ON）かかっています。Bさんはどこに住んでいますか？（想像上の住所で可）— 彼は熊本（IN）坪井（IN）3番地に（AT）住んでいます。*
彼は今、学校に（at）います。
    in Kumamoto.（熊本に）
    in Kumamoto Ken.（熊本県に）
    in Kyusyu.（九州に）
    in Japan.（日本に）
    in the Orient.（東洋に）

魚はどこに住んでいますか？ — 鳥はどこでさえずっていますか？ — 魚は水の中に（IN）棲み、鳥は木の中で（IN）さえずっています。（魚が水に囲まれているように、鳥は葉に囲まれているため、IN を用いる。）
鳥を見たら、It is ON the branches, &c.（枝の上に（ON）いる）などと言うこともできます。蟬を見たとき、There is a semi ON that tree.（あの木に蟬がいます。）と言います。ただし、蟬の鳴き声は聞こえるけれども姿が見えないときは、IN the tree と言います。蟋蟀は草むらの中で（IN）歌っています。草が蟋蟀を隠し、取り囲んでいます。
ただし、奇妙な例外もあります。:— 鏡を（IN）覗き込むと、何が見えますか？

* これは「彼は、熊本（という市）に住んでいます」の場合は in を、「彼は坪井（という地域）に住んでいます」の場合は in を、「彼は3番地に住んでいます」の場合は at を用いよ、ということである。

you see? — I see my own face IN the looking-glass. (This is against the rule.) Why do we say "in"? — Because the looking-glass deceives the eye. We do not see the real surface, but seem to be looking into another room or place. There are very few such exceptions; but all polished surfaces may be spoken of in the same way.

Look at a boat ON the water. How many shadows has it? —— It has two: the colored shadow is IN the boat, the shadow which has no color is ON the water.

Where do the children play? —— They play IN the street.

Where is the chair? —— The chair is IN the corner. (A corner is enclosed on three sides.) IN one tree there was a bird, IN another there was a squirrel.

If with Tenses

If —— is ——, is —— or will ——
If —— was ——, would ——
If —— had been ——, would have ——
If —— would ——, should ——
 —— should ——, would ——

you see? I see my own face IN the looking-glass. (This is against the rule.) Why do we say "in"? Because the looking-glass deceives the eye. We do not see the real surface, but seem to be looking into another room or place. There are very few such exceptions; but all polished surfaces may be spoken of in the same way.

Look at a boat ON the water. How many shadows has it? — It has two: the colored shadow is IN the boat, the shadow which has no color is ON the water.

Where do the children play? — They play IN the street.

Where is the chair? — The chair is IN the corner. (A corner is enclosed on three sides.) IN one tree there was a bird, IN another there was a squirrel.

鏡の中に自分の顔が見えます。（これはルールに反する使い方。）なぜ in を使うのでしょうか？なぜなら、鏡は目を欺くものだからです。私たちは本当の表面を見ているのではありませんが、鏡の向こうにはもう1つ別の部屋または場所があるように見えます。例外はほとんどないのですが、磨き上げられた表面については、すべて同じように表現します。

水の上の（ON）ボートを見てください。影はいくつありますか？ー2つあります：色の着いた影はボートの中（IN）、色のついていない影が水の上に（ON）あります。

子どもたちはどこで遊びますか？ー道路で（IN）遊びます。

椅子はどこにありますか？ー椅子はその隅に（IN）あります。（隅は3面に囲まれている。）ある木には（IN）鳥、別の木には（IN）リスがいました。

If with Tenses

If ____ is ____, is ____ or will ____
If ____ was ____, would ____
If ____ had been ____, would have ____
If ____ would ____, should ____
____ should ____, would ____

If と時制

If ____ is ____, is ____ or will ____
If ____ was ____, would ____
If ____ had been ____, would have ____
If ____ would ____, should ____
____ should ____, would ____

Rules of Shall and Will

1. I will ———— determination
2. Thou shalt ⎫
3. He shall ⎬ must

1. We will ———— determination
* 2. You shall ⎫ must
3. They shall ⎬ obligation

1. I shall
2. Thou wilt
3. He will   ⎱ Simple future
1. We shall
* 2. You will   Notice:— A mistake in this rule of the first person is not very bad. * But a mistake in the 2nd person plural is <u>very bad</u>.
3. They will

Exercises on "Will" and "Shall"

"I SHALL go to school tomorrow."
"He WILL go to school tomorrow."
"Where WILL you go tomorrow?"
"WILL you come to see me?"

Please give an example of { resolve / command } by the use of the future, 3rd person singular.

"He SHALL die, because he has committed

Rules of Shall and Will

1. I will _____ determination
2. Thou shalt ⎫
3. He shall   ⎬ must

1. We will _____ determination
*2. You shall ⎫
3. They shall ⎬ must / obligation

1. I shall   ⎫
2. Thou wilt ⎪
3. He will   ⎬ Simple future
1. We shall   ⎪   Notice: — A mistake in this rule of the first person is not very bad. *But a mistake in the 2nd person plural is very bad.
*2. You will ⎪
3. They will ⎭

Exercises on "Will" and "Shall"

"I SHALL go to school tomorrow."
"He WILL go to school tomorrow."
"Where WILL you go tomorrow?"
"WILL you come to see me?"
Please give an example of { resolve / command } by the use of the future, 3rd person singular.
"He SHALL die, because he has committed

Shall と Will のルール

1．私は〜するつもりだ－決心
2．あなたは〜すべきだ ⎫
3．彼は〜すべきだ   ⎬ 義務

1．私たちは〜するつもりだ－決心
*2．あなたは〜すべきだ ⎫
3．彼らは〜すべきだ   ⎬ 義務／責務

1．私は〜するだろう   ⎫ 単純未来
2．あなたは〜するだろう ⎪ 注：一人称のルールを間違ってもそれほど悪くはありません。
3．彼は〜するだろう   ⎬ *しかし、二人称複数形の間違いはたいへん悪い。
1．私たちは〜するだろう ⎪
*2．あなたは〜するだろう⎪
3．彼らは〜するだろう ⎭

Will と Shall の練習

明日、私は学校へ行くだろう。（SHALL）
明日、彼は学校へ行くだろう。（WILL）
明日、あなたはどこへ行きますか？（WILL）
私に会いに来てくれますか？（WILL）
決意／命令を表す例題を、三人称単数未来形を使って示しなさい。
彼は犯罪を犯したため、死ななければならない。（SHALL）

a crime."
("You SHALL obey, or you SHALL be put in prison.")

Ex—— Great Britain said to the American colonies, "Pay your taxes!" "We WILL not," said the colonies. "You SHALL," said Great Britain. And then there was war!

"An English judge says to a prisoner, 'You SHALL be hanged by the neck until you are dead, and may God have mercy on your soul!'"

You ask me to go with you to Suizenji. But what can one see at Suizenji? What SHALL we do there?   We SHALL amuse ourselves; and there WILL be many friends of ours there.

Do you think anybody WILL be at school tomorrow?   Yes; I think we SHALL all be at school.

WILL you be so kind as to lend me your book?   Yes, I SHALL be very glad to lend it to you. (In this case "Will you" implies the possible WILL of the person asked. But "would you" is

a crime."
("You SHALL obey, or you SHALL be put in prison.")
Ex – Great Britain said to the American colonies, "Pay your taxes!" "We WILL not," said the colonies. "You SHALL," said Great Britain. And then there was war!

An English judge says to a prisoner, "You SHALL be hanged by the neck until you are dead, and may God have mercy on your soul!"

You ask me to go with you to Suizenji. But what can one see at Suizenji? What SHALL we do there? We SHALL amuse ourselves; and there WILL be many friends of ours there.

Do you think anybody WILL be at school tomorrow? Yes; I think we SHALL all be at school.

WILL you be so kind as to lend me your book? Yes, I SHALL be very glad to lend it to you. (In this case "will you" implies the possible WILL of the person asked. But "would you" is

（命令に従いなさい（SHALL）。さもないと、牢屋に入れます（SHALL）。）
例－イギリスは、アメリカにあった植民地に言いました。「税金を払いなさい！」すると、植民地は「払うつもりはない（WILL）」と言いました。イギリスは「払え（SHALL）」と言います。そして戦争が起きました。

イギリス人の裁判官が囚人に向かって言いました。「絞首刑に処す（SHALL）。お前の魂に神のご加護のあらんことを！」

水前寺へ一緒に行こうと誘ってくれましたね。ところで、水前寺の見所は何でしょう？ 私たちは、そこで何をしますか（SHALL）？ 楽しく過ごすことになるでしょう（SHALL）。それに、そこには友だちがたくさんいるでしょうから（WILL）。

明日、みんな学校に来るかな（WILL）？
うん、みんな学校に来ると思うよ（SHALL）。

あなたの本を貸して下さいませんか（WILL）？
ええ、喜んでお貸しいたします（SHALL）。
（この場合、will you は尋ねられた人の可能な意思（WILL）を意味する。would you を用いると、より丁寧になる。）

still more polite.)

What do you think WILL be the condition of the Japanese merchants in another 50 years? —— I think that they WILL become very, very rich. Then you think the national commerce WILL continue to increase? —— Yes, I am sure that it WILL. (Never say "he shall," "it shall," "You shall," "they shall," —— unless you mean "must.")

Exclamatory phrases end with ! . Questions or interrogative sentences end with ? .

Mark of exclamation

Question Mark

Rules for exclamatory phrases : —— the order is this:
1st : the exclamatory words
2nd : the adjective (if there is any adjective)
3rd : the subject (noun or pronoun)
   (together with article if a noun)
4th : and last, the verb.

When there are both noun and adjective, the article may often go before the adjective

1	2	3	4
Exclam. words	adjective	subject	verb
How	rainy	the weather	is !
What	a gloomy	sky !	
Oh, how	sorry	we	feel !
Ah, what	beautiful	weather	it is !

still more polite.)

What do you think WILL be the condition of the Japanese merchants in another 50 years? — I think that they WILL become very, very rich. Then you think the national commerce WILL continue to increase? — Yes, I am sure that it WILL. (Never say "he shall," "it shall," "you shall", "they shall," — unless you mean "must.")

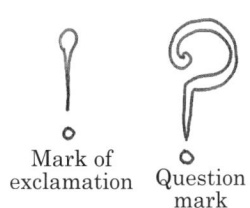

Mark of exclamation   Question mark

Exclamatory phrases end with !
Questions or interrogative sentences end with ?

Rules for exclamatory phrases: — the order is this:

When there are both noun and adjective, the article may often go before the adjective

1st: the exclamatory words
2nd: the adjective (if there is any adjective)
3rd: the subject (noun or pronoun)
    (together with article if a noun)
4th: and last, the verb.

1 Exclam.words	2 adjective	3 subject	4 verb
How	rainy	the weather	is!
What	a gloomy	sky!	
Oh, how	sorry	we	feel!
Ah, what	beautiful	weather	it is!

これから50年後の日本の商人たちはどうなっていると思いますか（WILL）？とても、とてもお金持ちになっていると思います（WILL）。それで、あなたは国の貿易は引き続き成長すると思いますか（WILL）？はい、そう考えています。（「せねばならぬ」の意味を伝えるのでなければ、he shall や it shall、you shall、they shall は用いてはならない。）

感嘆符   疑問符

感嘆文は！で終わります。
疑問文は？で終わります。

感嘆文のルール ― 順番は以下のとおり

名詞と形容詞の二つがある場合、冠詞は形容詞の前によく置かれます。
1：感嘆詞
2：形容詞（形容詞がある場合）
3：主語（名詞または代名詞）（名詞の場合は、冠詞を伴う）
4：最後は動詞

1．感嘆詞	2．形容詞	3．主語	4．動詞
何という	雨降りな	天気	なのだ！
何という	陰気な	空！	
*おー、何て	申し訳なく	私たちは	感じる！
あー、何て	美しい	天気	なのだ！

*　日本語らしく訳せば「あー、なんとも申し訳ない気持ちです」になる。

Rules for questions or interrogative phrases.

The verbs come after the words "How", "How many", "Why", "What", "Which", &c—— instead of at the end of the sentence. When there is an interrogative pronoun at the beginning of the question, the noun it modifies may follow it as "What kind of tree is it?"

Why did you do it?
Where are you going?
When did you come here?
Which book have you?
What do you say?
Which is your opinion?
How blue the sky is!
Is the sky blue?
How useful the study is!
Is the study useful?   or
How is the study useful?

Subject — Kumamoto

When did you come to Kumamoto?
Where is Kumamoto?
How large is Kumamoto?
What is the population of Kumamoto?
Which part do you live in?

The word "congratulate" can never be used of

Rules for questions or interrogative phrases	疑問文のルール
The verbs come after the words "How," "How many," "Why," "What," "Which," &c ___ instead of at the end of the sentence. When there is an interrogative pronoun at the beginning of the question, the noun it modifies may follow it as "What kind of tree is it?"	動詞は文章の最後ではなく、HowやHow many、Why、What、Whichなどの後に続きます。疑問代名詞が疑問文のはじめにある場合、それが修飾する名詞はその後に来ます。
	What kind of tree is it?
	（その木の種類は何ですか？）
Why did you do it?	なぜ、それをしたのですか？
Where are you going?	どこへ行くのですか？
When did you come here?	いつ、ここに来たのですか？
Which book have you?	どの本を持っていますか？
What do you say?	何と言いますか？
Which is your opinion?	あなたの意見はどちらですか？
How blue the sky is!	空はなんと青いんだろう！
Is the sky blue?	空は青いですか？
How useful the study is!	勉強は、なんて有益なものなんだろう！
Is the study useful? or	勉強は役立ちますか？ または
How is the study useful?	勉強はどのように役立ちますか？

Subject – Kumamoto

主題 – 熊本

When did you come to Kumamoto?	いつ、熊本に来ましたか？
Where is Kumamoto?	熊本はどこですか？
How large is Kumamoto?	熊本はどのくらいの大きさですか？
What is the population of Kumamoto?	熊本の人口はどのくらいですか？
Which part do you live in?	（熊本の）どのあたりに住んでいますか？

The word "congratulate" can never be used of

congratulate（祝う）という言葉を「物」に使うことはありません。

things. You can congratulate a person, — but never a thing. Why?

Congratulate ⎯⎯ from Latin "con"   "gratulate"
                            with   to be glad, to be happy.
"I congratulate you" means "I am glad with you", or "I am happy because you are happy". But you can only say to a person, not to a thing. We congratulate persons, not days or things or events. (No preposition is used after this word.)

Things or events are CELEBRATED. They cannot be congratulated.

Sympathize (with) ⎯⎯ from Greek: sum "with";
                              patheia "to suffer".
"I sympathize with you." ⎯⎯ "I suffer with you."

Why did the students give an entertainment on Friday evening? ⎯⎯ They gave an entertainment to CELEBRATE the anniversary of the Imperial Wedding. The nobility of Tokyo visited the palace to congratulate Their Majesties.

Have you seen the new postage-stamps printed in honor of the festival? ⎯⎯ Yes, I have seen them. What is the English inscription upon them?

IMPERIAL WEDDING 25 ANNIVERSARY

Why 25 anniversary? Should it not have been 25th anniversary? ⎯⎯ Yes, but there was no

things. You can congratulate a person, – but never a thing. Why?
Congratulate – from Latin "con" "gratulate"
with to be glad, to be happy

"I congratulate you" means "I am glad with you", or "I am happy because you are happy". But you can only say to a person, not to a thing. We congratulate persons, not days or things or events. (No preposition is used after this word.)

 Things or events are CELEBRATED. They cannot be congratulated.

Sympathize (with) – from Greek: sum "with",
patheia "to suffer".
"I sympathize with you." – "I suffer with you."

 Why did the students give an entertainment on Friday evening? – They gave an entertainment to CELEBRATE the anniversary of the Imperial Wedding. The nobility of Tokyo visited the palace to congratulate Their Majesties.

 Have you seen the new postage-stamps printed in honor of the festival? – Yes, I have seen them. What is the English inscription upon them?
IMPERIAL WEDDING 25 ANNIVERSARY
Why 25 anniversary? Should it not have been 25th anniversary? – Yes, but there was no

人を祝うものであり、物を祝うものではないからです。その理由は？
Congratulate－ラテン語のcon（一緒に）とgratulate（喜ぶ、幸せです）に由来します。
I congratulate you は、I am glad with you（私はあなたとともに喜びます。）またはI am happy because you are happy.（あなたが幸せだから、私も幸せです）という意味です。congratulateは人に対しては言えても物に対しては言えません。人を祝うのであり、月日や物、イベントを祝うときに使う言葉ではありません。（この単語のあとに前置詞は用いない。）
物やイベントは、CELEBRATEDを用います。これらは祝福してあげられないものだからです。

Sympathize (with)－ギリシア語のsum（一緒に）とpatheia（耐え忍ぶ）に由来します。
I sympathize with you.（同情します。）－I suffer with you.（あなたとともに耐え忍びます。）

なぜ、学生は金曜日の晩に催し物を行ったのですか？－学生たちは、天皇・皇后両陛下のご成婚二十五周年を祝う（CELEBRATE）ために催し物を開きました。東京にいる貴族は皇居を訪れ、両陛下にお祝いを述べました。
祝典を記念して印刷された新しい郵便切手を見ましたか？－はい、見ました。切手に書いてある英語は何と読むのですか？
天皇皇后両陛下御成婚二十五周年祝典
なぜ、25 anniversaryなのでしょう？本来なら、25th anniversaryではありませんか？

room for more letters. [I have not enough room on the board to write more.]

To-day is Tuesday, the 13th of March, the twenty-seventh year of Meiji.

Rules:——

When the day is mentioned first, "of" should be used before the word "month":—— "the 25th of June." But when the month is mentioned first, it is different:—— "June (the) 25th, the 27th year of Meiji." So we can also write:—— "March (the) 13th, the 27th year of Meiji."

What kind of entertainment was given by the students?—— They gave a very nice DRAMATIC entertainment. Most of the pieces were COMEDIES (or were comic).

What is a play called which makes people weep?—— A tragedy.

1. Play (<u>asobi</u>) is an abstract noun, and has no plural.
Ex.—— I like to see the innocent play of children. (the word "games" may be used for a plural.)

2. Play (theatrical)—— a drama of any kind. (This is a common noun.)

    The PLAYS of Shakespeare
    The PLAYS of Molière.

Why did the peasants in the play become angry with the surveyors?—— Because the surveyors room for more letters. [I have not enough room on the board to write more.]

To-day is Tuesday, the 13th of March, the twenty-seventh year of Meiji.

Rules: —

When the day is mentioned first, "of" should be used before the word "month." — "the 25th of June." But when the month is mentioned first, it is different. — "June (the) 25th, the 27th year of Meiji." So we can also write: — "March (the) 13th, the 27th year of Meiji."

What kind of entertainment was given by the students? — They gave a very nice DRAMATIC entertainment. Most of the pieces were COMEDIES (or were comic).

What is a play called which makes people weep? — A tragedy.

1. Play (<u>asobi</u>) is an abstract noun, and has no plural.
Ex — I like to see the innocent play of children. (the word "games" may be used for a plural.)
2. Play (theatrical) — a drama of any kind. (This is a common noun.)
    The PLAYS of Shakespeare
    The PLAYS of Molière

Why did the peasants in the play become angry with the surveyors? — Because the surveyors

――― そうですね。どうやら文字を入れるスペースがなかったようです。［黒板に、これ以上書くスペースがありません。］
今日は明治27年3月13日、火曜日です。

ルール：－

日付が先に記されている場合、of が month（月）の前に用いられます。－ the 25th of June.（6月25日）ただし、月が先に記されている場合は異なります。－ June (the) 25th, the 27th year of Meiji.（明治27年6月25日）次のようにも表せます：－ March (the) 13th, the 27th year of Meiji.（明治27年3月13日）

どんな出し物を学生たちは行ったのですか？－彼らはとても素敵な劇の出し物を行いました。大半の出し物はコメディ（喜劇風）でした。

観る人に涙を流させる演劇は、何と呼ばれていますか？－悲劇と呼ばれています。

1．Play（遊び）は抽象名詞であり、複数形はありません。
例－子どもたちの無邪気な遊びを見るのが好きです。（複数形のときは、games を用いると良い。）
2．Play（演劇）－あらゆる種類の戯曲。（これは普通名詞です。）
The PLAYS of Shakespeare（シェイクスピアの戯曲）
The PLAYS of Molière（モリエールの戯曲）

なぜ劇の中で、農民は測量技師に怒ったのですか？－測量技師が作物を傷つけたからです。

were injuring the crops.

When a man has been dead for a long time, we never say "Mr. ___."

I ask‿you a question.
    Many students use "to" after "ask". Never say "ask to." That is French — not English.

Obey: ___ I will obey‿my parents.
    no preposition. Never say "obey to."
That is French — not English. But after "obedient" which is an adjective, we use "to."
    "Children are OBEDIENT TO their parents."

The verb "go" with prepositions: ___ "to," "with," "up," "down," "by," "from," "beside," "under," "over," "across," "through," "before," "behind," "in," "into," "away," "along," "after."

Examples: ___
I will go TO Suizenji.
I am glad to go WITH you.
I shall go UP this mountain (the stairs).
Every day I go BY the house, and I see my friend at the door. ("To go by" (in this sense) means "to pass in front of." "By" may also mean "past.")
Time goes BY fast.

were injuring the crops.
    When a man has been dead for a long time, we never say "Mr. ——."

    I ask ∧ you a question.
    many students use "to" after "ask." Never say "ask to." That is French – not English.
Obey: – I will obey ∧ my parents.
         no preposition Never say "obey to".
That is French – not English. But after "obedient" which is an adjective, we use "to".
    "Children are OBEDIENT TO their parents."

    The verb "go" with prepositions: – "to", "with", "up", "down", "by", "from", "beside", "under", "over", "across", "through", "before", "behind", "in", "into", "away", "along", "after".

Examples: –
    I will go TO Suizenji.
    I am glad to go WITH you.
    I shall go UP this mountain (the stairs)
    Every day I go BY the house, and I see my friend at the door. ("To go by" (in this sense) means "to pass in front of." "By" may also mean "past".)
    Time goes BY fast.

亡くなって長期の時間が経った人に対して、Mr. —— を用いることはありません。

質問をします。
ask のあとに to を使う学生が多いですが、ask to と言ってはいけません。それはフランス語であり、英語ではありません。
Obey（従う）：－ 私は両親の言うことに従います。ここでは前置詞なし。けっして obey to としてはならない。それはフランス語であり、－英語ではない。しかし形容詞の obedient の後には to を用います。
Children are OBEDIENT TO their parents.（子どもたちは両親の言うことに従います。）

動詞 go と前置詞：－ to, with, up, down, by, from, beside, under, over, across, through, before, behind, in, into, away, along, after.

例：－
水前寺に（TO）行きます。
あなたと一緒に（WITH）行くことができて嬉しいです。
この山（階段）をのぼりましょう。（UP）
私は毎日、その家のそばを（BY）通り、ドアのところで友だちと会っています。（To go by はここでは to pass in front of（前を通り過ぎる）を表します。By には past（過ぎる）の意味も含まれます。）
時間は速く過ぎます。（BY）

The River Shirakawa flows BY.
I went FROM Kumamoto TO Nagasaki.
I went BESIDE the tree.
After "go" the preposition must be "into", not "in" _____ unless the place is not mentioned.
I went INTO the house. (place mentioned)
He called me, and I went IN (no place mentioned)
I went INTO the river (place mentioned)
The water looked cool, I went IN and swam. (no place mentioned)

General rule :—
After verbs of motion we use "into", when the idea is of entering any enclosed space.
"I went INTO the field."

Across (motion over a surface from one side to another)

Across (motion over a surface from one side to another)

Through (penetration) motion passing into and through a body.) — He passed a sword THROUGH the man

Exercises on the Articles

a weak "form" of "that" "those" &c.
The

A or An
"one"

The River Shirakawa flows BY.
I went FROM Kumamoto TO Nagasaki.
I went BESIDE the tree.

After "go" the preposition must be "into," not "in" – unless the place is not mentioned.

I went INTO the house. (place mentioned)
He called me, and I went IN (no place mentioned)
I went INTO the river. (place mentioned)
The water looked cool, I went IN and swam. (no place mentioned)

General rule: –

After verbs of motion we use "into", when the idea is of entering any enclosed space. –
"I went INTO the field."

Across (motion over a surface from one side to another)

Across (motion over a surface from one side to another)

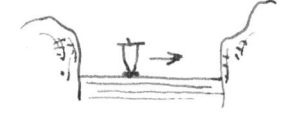

Through (penetration,) motion passing into and through a body.

"He passed a sword THROUGH the man"

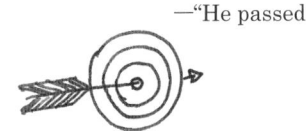

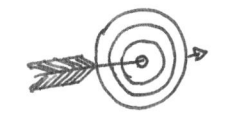

Exercises on the Articles

The
=
a weak form
of
"that" "those" &c.

A or An
=
"one"

General rule: —— Before every common noun in the singular, some article must be put, or else a stronger modifier, —— such as "that" or "one", &c.

Before the following no article is used: ——
1. Abstract nouns. These are names of qualities.
2. Material nouns. These are names of substances.
3. Proper names.

What is good to eat when we are hungry?
When we are hungry EVERY thing is good to eat. (No article is used before THING, because EVERY is a stronger demonstrative.)
What do you have for breakfast?
We have BREAD for breakfast. (Bread is a material noun, —— so no article is used.)
What is the highest virtue of a soldier?
COURAGE is the highest virtue of a soldier. (Courage being an abstract noun, no article is used. But we say "the highest virtue" in order to limit the meaning of the word to a particular kind of virtue.)

Examples of this Modification or Particularization: ——

Abstract	Abstract Particularization
What is the most destructive element?	What happened to the city of Kumamoto in the 10th year of Meiji?
The most destructive element is FIRE.	There was a war, and Kumamoto was destroyed by A GREAT FIRE.

General rule: — Before every common noun in the singular, some article must be put, or else a stronger modifier, — such as "that" or "one", &c.

Before the following no article is used: —
1. Abstract nouns. These are names of qualities.
2. Material nouns. These are names of substances.
3. Proper names.

What is good to eat when we are hungry?
When we are hungry EVERY thing is good to eat. (No article is used before THING, because EVERY is a stronger demonstrative.)
What do you have for breakfast?
We have BREAD for breakfast. (Bread is a material noun, —— so no article is used.)
What is the highest virtue of a soldier?
COURAGE is the highest virtue of a soldier. (Courage being an abstract noun, no article is used. But we say "the highest virtue" in order to limit the meaning of the word to a particular kind of virtue.)

Examples of this Modification or Particularization: —

Abstract	Abstract Particularization
What is the most destructive element?	What happened to the city of Kumamoto in the 10th year of Meiji?
The most destructive element is FIRE.	There was a war, and Kumamoto was destroyed by A GREAT FIRE.

一般的ルール：－単数形の普通名詞の前には何らかの冠詞が置かれます。もしくは、that や one などの、より指示性の強い修飾語が必ず置かれます。

以下の例では冠詞は必要ありません：－
1．抽象名詞：これは質を表す名詞です。
2．物質名詞：これは物質の名称です。
3．固有名詞

お腹が空いたときは何を食べたら良いでしょう？　お腹が空いたら、何でも食べていいんですよ。（Every（何でも）が強い指示詞なので、THING の前に冠詞は不要。）
朝食は何を食べますか？
朝食はパンです。（Bread は物質名詞のため、－冠詞は不要。）
兵士にとって最も大切な美徳とは何ですか？
勇気が兵士にとって最も大切な美徳です。（Courage（勇気）は抽象名詞のため、冠詞は不要。ただし、この語の意味を特定の種類の virtue（美徳）に限定させるため、the highest virtue とする。）

修飾または特定化の例：－

抽象	抽象的な詳述
最も大きな破壊的要因は何ですか？	明治10年、熊本市に何が起こりましたか？
最も大きな破壊的要因は火です。	戦争があり、そのときの大火で熊本は破壊されました。

Abstract or Material	The same —— Particularization
What are the desks made of?	Is <u>the</u> wood of the desks hard or soft? It is <u>a</u> very hard wood. (or <u>The</u> wood is hard.)
They are made of <u>wood</u>. (Material noun — no article)	
What kind of <u>water</u> is there at Suizenji?	<u>The</u> water at Suizenji is clear, fresh water.
What was Confucius famous for? For <u>wisdom</u>.	The wisdom of Confucius was very remarkable.
What makes the ground all white in winter? <u>Snow</u>. (m. n)	<u>The</u> snow last year was very light.
What do we study hard? To get knowledge (abstract)	Whose knowledge was great in ancient times? <u>The</u> knowledge of Socrates was great; —— that of Confucius was great.
What is <u>history</u>? History is the record of human action (abstract)	What history do you like best? I like <u>the</u> history of Japan best.

Abstract or Material	The same — Particularization	抽象または物質	同様－特定化
What are the desks made of?	Is <u>the</u> wood of the desks hard or soft? It is <u>a</u> very hard wood.	その机は何でできていますか？	その机の木は堅いですか、それとも軟らかいですか？
They are made of <u>wood</u>. (Material noun – no article)	(or <u>The</u> wood is hard.)	<u>木材</u>でできています。（物質名詞―冠詞なし）	とても堅い木材です。（<u>その</u>木材は堅いものです。）
What kind of <u>water</u> is there at Suizenji?	<u>The</u> water at Suizenji is clear, fresh water.	水前寺の<u>水</u>の種類は何ですか？	水前寺の水はきれいな真水です。
What was Confucius famous for? For <u>wisdom</u>.	<u>The</u> wisdom of Confucius was very remarkable.	孔子は何で有名でしたか？ <u>智恵</u>で有名でした。	孔子の智恵はたいへんすぐれたものでした。
What makes the ground all white in winter? Snow. (m.n)	<u>The</u> snow last year was very light.	冬、地面を真っ白にするものは何ですか？ 雪です。（物質名詞）	去年の雪はとても少なかった。
Why do we study hard? To get knowledge (abstract)	Whose knowledge was great in ancient times? <u>The</u> knowledge of Socrates was great; — that of Confucius was great.	なぜ、一生懸命勉強するのですか？ 知識（抽象名詞）を得るためです。	古代では誰の教えが偉大でしたか？ ソクラテスの教えです；－孔子の教えです。
What is <u>history</u>? History is the record of human action (abstract)	What history do you like best? I like <u>the</u> history of Japan best.	<u>歴史</u>とは何ですか？ 歴史は、人間の活動（抽象名詞）の記録です。	何の歴史が一番好きですか？ 私は日本史が一番好きです。

Exceptions to General Rules of the Article "the"

<u>The</u> sky	The weather
sea, ocean	The air or atmosphere
earth, world, globe	The ground
sun	<u>The</u> always before the name
moon	of a river.
stars	

Note: —— Never, never, NEVER put the article "the" before "Mount" or "Mt." —— as "Mount Aso" or "Mt. Fuji". In such cases "Mount" or "Mt." is part of the proper name, —— just as "Mr." is part of a proper name. It is just as wrong to say "The Mt. Aso" as it would be to say "The Mr. Nishimura". But before "mountain" always, always, ALWAYS put "the". —— "The mountain of Aso."

Examples: ——
The mountain of Kirishima is the highest in Kyushu. (or "Mount Kirishima" is ......, or "Mt. Kirishima" is .....).
The River Chikugo is the largest in Kyushu. (or The Chikugo is the largest river in Kyushu.)

Note: —— After "mountain" we generally use the preposition "of": —— "The mountain of Daisen". But "of" is not used after the word "river" ——

Exceptions to General Rules of the Article "the"

* <u>The</u> sky
    sea, ocean
    earth, world, globe
    sun
    moon
    stars

The weather
The air or atmosphere
The ground
<u>The</u> always before the name of a river.

Note: — Never, never, NEVER put the article "the" before "Mount" or "Mt." — as "Mount Aso" or "Mt. Fuji". In such cases "Mount" or "Mt." is part of the proper name, — just as "Mr." is part of a proper name. It is just as wrong to say "The Mt. Aso" as it would be to say "The Mr. Nishimura". But before "mountain" always, always, ALWAYS put "the". — "The mountain of Aso."

Examples: —
  The mountain of Kirishima is the highest in Kyushu. (or "Mount Kirishima" is…, or "Mt. Kirishima" is…).
  The River Chikugo is the largest in Kyushu. (or The Chikugo is the largest river in Kyushu.)

Note: — After "mountain" we generally use the preposition "of": — "The mountain of Daisen." But "of" is not used after the word "river" —

* <u>The</u> sky とあるが、これはそれに引続いて書かれた sea, ocean, earth, world, globe, sun, moon, stars の場合にも定冠詞 the をつける、ということを示す例示である。

定冠詞 the の一般的ルールの例外

空
海、大洋
地球、世界、地球
太陽
月
星

天候
空気または大気
大地
川の名前の前ではいつも <u>the</u>

注：— Mount や Mt. の前に決して the を置いてはいけません。— Mount Aso、Mt. Fuji. のようにすること。このような場合、Mount や Mt. は固有名詞の一部となります。— それはちょうど Mr. が固有名詞の一部であるのと同じようなものです。The Mt. Aso とするのは、The Mr. Nishimura にするようなもので、誤りです。
ただし、mountain の前にはいつも常に the を置きます。—The mountain of Aso.

例：—
The mountain of Kirishima is the highest in Kyushu.（霧島は九州で最も高い山です。）（または、Mount Kirishima is…、Mt. Kirishima is… でも可。）
The River Chikugo is the largest in Kyushu.（筑後川は九州で最も川幅が広いです。）（または、The Chikugo is the largest river in Kyushu. でも可。）

注：— mountain の後には通常、前置詞 of を使います。— The mountain of Daisen.（大山）
ただし、river の後には of は用いません —

before a proper name, except in speaking of an imaginary river.

The river of Oblivion (forgetfulness)
The River of the Three Roads (sanzu-no-kawa)
The River of Lamentation
The River of Tears

But in speaking of real rivers we say "the River Mississippi" —— not of Mississippi.

In Kyushu <u>the</u> climate is very good.
Today <u>the</u> weather is very fine.
The wind makes a musical sound in the pine-trees.
Grasshoppers live in <u>the</u> grass. (Before "grass" we also use the word "the".)
Coal is found deep in <u>the</u> ground.
<u>The moon</u> is the most beautiful sight in autumn.
An old story in words of one syllable to explain the common uses of the articles.
Once there was <u>a</u> good old man who lived in <u>a</u> far place. He used to earn <u>the</u> means to live by his skill to cut wood. While he worked in the hills, his wife stayed at home and wove.
One day <u>the</u> old man found in the hills <u>a</u>

(annotations: "one" above "a"; "that means by which he could live" beside "the means to live"; "that same old man" below "the old man"; "one" below final "a") before a proper name, except in speaking of an imaginary river.

The river of oblivion (forgetfulness)
The River of the Three Roads (sanzu-no-kawa)
The River of Lamentation
The River of Tears

But in speaking of real rivers we say "the River Mississippi" —— not of Mississippi.

In Kyushu <u>the</u> climate is very good.
Today <u>the</u> weather is very fine.
The wind makes a musical sound in the pine-trees.
Grasshoppers live in <u>the</u> grass. (Before "grass" we also use the word "the")
Coal is found deep in <u>the</u> ground.
<u>The</u> <u>moon</u> is the most beautiful sight in autumn.
An old story in words of one syllable to explain the common uses of the articles.
Once there was <u>a</u> good old man who lived
          (one)
in <u>a</u> far place. He used to earn <u>the</u> means to live
by his skill to cut wood. While he (that means by
                         which he could
worked in the hills, his wife stayed at home and live)
wove.

One day <u>the</u> old man found in the hills <u>a</u>
     (that same old man)   (one)

固有名詞の前で、想像上の河川を言う場合は別です。

The river of oblivion（forgetfulness）（忘却の川）
The River of the Three Roads（三途の川）
The River of Lamentation（嘆きの川）
The Rive of Tears（涙の川）

しかし実在する川については、of Mississippiではなく、the River Mississippi（ミシシッピ川）と言います。

九州では、気候はとてもいいです。
今日は、天気がとても良い。
風が松の木の間で音楽のような心地よい音を奏でています。
バッタは草むらに住んでいます。（grassの前には the を用いる。）
石炭は地中深くで見つかります。
月は、秋の季節で最も美しい眺めです。
１音節の語で冠詞の一般的な使い方を説明する昔話です。
昔、ある遠く離れた土地に一人の心優しいおじいさんが住んでいました。彼は、木を伐る技で生計を立てていました。（生計とはそれによって暮らすてだての意味です。）
彼が山で働いている間、おばあさんは家に残り、機織りをしていました。
ある日のこと、おじいさん（最初に登場した同じおじいさん）は丘の上である（一つの）

clear spring. He felt great thirst, as he had worked
hard that day, so he drank of the spring. When he
had drunk, he found he was [that same spring] not the same as
he had been. He had grown quite young. It was
the spring of youth at which he had drunk.
[that particular spring called—] He ran home and told his wife. The old wife
cried, "I too must drink of that spring, [that same] and get young
once more. Do you wait here, while I go?"

She went but did not come back. The old
man went to look for her. He reached [that same old man we have been talking]
the spring, and there he found no one but a small [he],
[the same spring we have been talking of] small child. The old wife had drunk [one] too
much and so was [that same] changed into a child.

About verbs used wrongly by students.

Wish — I wish to go to Suizenji. (Before a verb "wish" requires "to" after it.)
    I wish for a book. ("wish" requires the preposition "for" after it before a noun.)

Never, NEVER say "I wish you to do, etc." This
is very wrong. Why is this wrong? Because it is a
command, and therefore rude. But we can say,
"I wish that you would be so kind as to do, etc."

Want — "want" can be used nearly like "wish".
    Its meaning is a little strong. But before a
    noun (except in idioms) no preposition follows it.
    I want money; and I want a horse.

clear spring. He felt great thirst, as he had worked hard that day, so he drank of the spring. When he had drunk, he found he was not the same as he had been. He had grown quite young. It was the spring of youth at which he had drunk. He ran home and told his wife. The old wife cried, "I too must drink of that spring, and get young once more. Do you wait here, while I go?"

<small>the (that same) / the same as (that same spring) / the spring (that particular spring called...) / The old wife (that same)</small>

She went but did not come back. The old man went to look for her. He reached the spring, and there he found no one but a small, small child. The old wife had drunk too much and so was changed into a child.

<small>The old (that same old man we have been talking of) / the spring (the same spring we have been talking of) / a small (one) / The old wife (that same)</small>

きれいな泉を見つけました。その日、彼は一生懸命働き、とても喉が渇いていたので、その泉（同じ泉）の水を飲みました。飲んだ時、おじいさんはそれまでの自分ではなくなってしまったことに気づきました。とても若返ってしまったのです。若返りの泉（と呼ばれる特別な泉）の水を、彼は飲んだのです。彼は走って家へ帰り、おばあさんに言いました。するとおばあさん（同じ人）は叫んで、「私もその泉の水を飲んでもう一度若返らなくっちゃ。私が出かけている間、ここで待っていてくださいよ。」と言いました。

彼女は出かけていったものの、戻ってくることはありませんでした。おじいさん（最初に述べた老人と同じ人）はおばあさんを探しに出かけました。泉（先に述べた同じ泉）にたどり着きましたが、そこには小さな小さな子ども以外、誰もおりません。おばあさん（先に述べたのと同じ人）が泉の水を飲み過ぎて、子どもに戻ってしまったのでした。

About verbs used wrongly by students.

Wish – I wish to go to Suizenji. *(Before a verb "wish" requires "to" after it.)*
I wish for a book. *("wish" requires the preposition "for" after it before a noun.)*

Never, NEVER say "I wish you to do, etc." This is very wrong. Why is this wrong? Because it is a command, and therefore rude. But we can say "I wish that you would be so kind as to do, etc."

Want – "want" can be used nearly like "wish." Its meaning is a little strong. But before a noun (except in idioms) no preposition follows it. I want money; and I want a horse.

学生が間違って使う動詞について

Wish（願う）－水前寺に行きたいです。（動詞の前にwishが来るときはwishの後にtoが必要）
本が欲しい。（wishは次に名詞が来るときはwishの後に前置詞forがその名詞の前に必要）

I wish you to do. などとは言わないこと。これはひどく間違った言い方です。なぜ間違いなのでしょう？ この使い方は命令を表すため、失礼な言い方になるからです。ただし、I wish that you would be so kind as to do.（親切にもそれをしてくださることを願います。）などのように表現することはできます。

Want（欲する）－ want は wish とほぼ同じように使うことができます。意味合いは少し強くなります。ただし、名詞の前（慣用句は除く）に前置詞は置かれません。
I want money.（お金がほしい）； I want a horse.（馬がほしい）

With a verb :—— I want to read your geography.
Remember that "want for" is an idiom only, and means "to be in need of"—— "to suffer because one has not got something." They want for food. (They are suffering from hunger.)

Examples of difference :——
I want a new hat. (= I would like to have a new hat.)
I want for a new hat. (= I am suffering because I have not a new hat.)

Ask —— (Never say "ask to") —— { Before the person no preposition
Before the object the prepositions "for" or "about" or "to" (with verb) }

May I ask you for a little money?
May I ask you to lend me a little money?

Say —— In Japanese after a speaker's words you say to iu —— but in English the rule is different. Never say "he said that" —— before the exact words of a speaker. Only use "that" when the meaning is given —— not the exact words.

Examples :——
Meaning only } He said that he was going to school.
Exact words he said } He said, "I am going to school."
Meaning } He said that the study of English was very difficult.
Exact words } He said, "The study of English is very difficult."

With a verb : – I <u>want to</u> read your geography.
Remember that "want for" is an idiom only, and means
"to be in need of" – "to suffer because one has not got
something". They want for food. (They are suffering
from hunger.)

Examples of difference : –
    I <u>want</u> a new hat. (= I would like to have a new hat.)
    I <u>want for</u> a new hat. (= I am suffering because I have
                        not got a new hat.)

Ask – (Never say "ask to") { Before the person <u>no preposition</u>
Before the object the prepositions "for" or "about" or "to" (with verb) }

May I ask you <u>for</u> a little money?
May I ask you <u>to</u> lend me a little money?

Say – In Japanese after a speaker's words you
    say <u>to iu</u> – but in English the rule is different.
    Never say "he said that" – before the exact words
    of a speaker. Only use "that" when the meaning
    is given – not the exact words.

Examples : –
Meaning only } He said that he was going to school.
Exact words he said } He said, "I am going to school."
Meaning } He said that the study of English was very difficult.
Exact words } He said, "The study of English is very difficult."

動詞とともに：– I <u>want to</u> read your geography.（あなたの地理の本を読みたい。）want for は慣用句のみの用法であり、to be in need of（必要である）の意味です。– つまり to suffer because one has not got something（何かを得ることができなくなって苦しむ）を意味します。They want for food.（彼らは食物不足で苦しんでいる。）

違いの例：–
I <u>want</u> a new hat.（= 新しい帽子がほしい。）
I <u>want for</u> a new hat.（= 新しい帽子が手に入らなかったので辛い思いをしている。）

Ask –（ask to とはけっして言わない。）人称の前では前置詞は不要。
目的語の前では前置詞は for または about、to（この場合は動詞と一緒に）が用いられます。
少しお金<u>を</u>お願いしても良いですか？
少しお金<u>を</u>お貸しいただいても良いですか？

Say – 日本語では話し手の言葉の後に「<u>と言う</u>」を付けます。– しかし、英語ではルールが異なります。he said that とは言いません。said の後には、話し手の生の直接的な言葉が来ます。that が使えるのは、話し手が話した内容を示すときに限ります。話し手の直接の話そのものではありません。

例：–
話の意味のみの場合：He said that he was going to school.（彼は学校へ行く旨言った。）
彼が言った直接の言葉：He said, "I am going to school."（彼は、「僕は学校へ行くところだ。」と言った。）
話の内容の場合：He said that the study of English was very difficult.（英語の勉強はとても難しい旨彼は言った。）
彼が言った直接の言葉：He said, "The study of English is very difficult."（彼は、「英語の勉強はとても難しい」と言った。）

Tell ——— Rule: ——— Before the object of "tell" no preposition.
"relates to" Sometimes "to" before the person.
tale (story) Better use no preposition with a direct object.
  "He told me a story."
Never say "tell to" when the sentence can be
understood without the preposition.

Examples of possible use: ———
  "Three of us had heard the same story at different
  times. John <u>to</u> whom it was first told, etc.,
  or, the first to tell it <u>to</u> us was, etc."
We leave out the "to" when we can, even in such
a sentence as, ———
  "The story told my brother, etc."
    ——— (instead of "told to my brother".)

Tell —Rule: — Before the object of "tell" no preposition
‖
(relates to
tale (story))
    Sometimes "to" before the person.
    Better use no preposition with a direct object.
    "He told me a story."
Never say "tell to" when the sentence can be understood without the preposition.

Examples of possible use: —
    "Three of us had heard the same story at different times. John to whom it was first told, etc.,
    or, the first to tell it to us was, etc."
We leave out the "to" when we can, even in such a sentence as, —
    "The story told my brother, etc."
    — (instead of "told to my brother.")

Tell（語り（物語）と関連する）— ルール：—
tell の目的語の前には前置詞は用いない。
ときどき、人称の前に to を置くことがあります。直接目的語のときは前置詞を用いないほうが良いでしょう。
He told me a story.（彼は私に物語を話してくれた。）
前置詞がなくても意味が通じる場合は、決して tell to としてはいけません。

考えられる例：—
私たち3人は同じ話を、それぞれ別の時に聞きました。最初に聞いたジョンは…など。初めてその話を私たちにしてくれたのは…など。以下のような文章の場合でも to は用いません。
The story told my brother, etc.（弟に話された話）—（told to my brother. にはならない。）

『熊本高校時代に於ける Lafcadio Hearn の英語教授』
の内容とその意義

西川盛雄

（1）背景

　ラフカディオ・ハーン（小泉八雲）は明治24年（1891）11月19日に松江から熊本に赴任して来た。第五高等中学校第3代校長嘉納治五郎の出迎えを春日駅（現熊本駅）で受け、熊本時代の第一歩を踏み出したのである。翌20日にはもう学校に出かけている。24日には就任式があり、この日から授業を始めている。熊本に来て暫くは旅館（不知火館）に投宿していたが、学校から提供された洋風の宿舎は断り、25日に手取本町34番地の赤星邸を借家として入り、本格的な熊本生活が始まったのである。

　滑り出しは順調なようであった。しかしこの時代はハーンにとっては必ずしも幸せな時代環境ではなかった。明治維新から20年以上経ち、復古主義が力を増し、富国強兵、殖産興業にもとづく欧化政策によって国力は増すものの時代は日清戦争に向かう中で軍事費が嵩み、国家的な緊縮財政が余儀なくされていた。そのため、国は節約を奨め、教育費にも手をつけ、国会では出来て間もない官制の5つの高等中学校のうち3つまでの廃止を議論するというきびしい時勢になっていたのである。第五高等中学校もその廃止の対象になっていた。それは同時にお雇い外国人として赴任したばかりのハーンには失職の不安が付きまとうことになる。西田千太郎への手紙（1892年12月13日付）でつぎのように書き記している。「ああ、再び野蛮な国会に直面しています。第五高等学校を含めて、3つの高等学校を廃止する提案とは！どうなろうとも夏以後ここにいないつもりです。あまりにも危険です」。

　ただでさえ身分の不安定な外国人教師の立場である。自らの不安定な身分的状況と当時の日本の高等教育制度の軽視を予感したハーンはたちまち不信と不安の渦に巻き込まれることになる。さらに熊本は明治10年（1877）の西南戦争により多くの神社仏閣をはじめ昔からの街並みも破壊されていた。そして勝利した官軍の新政府はこの地にあって急速に近代化・西洋化を遂げようとしていた。前任地の松江は10月は神在月と呼ばれ多くの神話に彩られたいわば〈神都〉と言うべき場所であったが、これに比して熊本は西南戦争後は〈軍都〉とも言うべき新たな近代的な町づくりを進めていた。さらに第五高等中学校の同僚たちは概ね明治新政府の欧化政策を押し進めるべく配置された人々であった。たとえば英語主任であった佐久間信恭は札幌農学校出身でウィリアム・クラークの薫陶を受けた人であり、また大倉（本田）増次郎は近くの回春病院でハンセン氏病患者の救済に当たっていたイギリス人宣教師リデルから英語を学び、泰西のキリスト教精神の影響を強く受け

た人であった。このような中で会津出身で戊辰戦争で敗北したが恩赦で罪が許され、やがて第一高等中学校を経て第五高等中学校に来た漢文・漢詩の教師で「神様のような風貌」を呈していた秋月胤永との出会いはハーンを大いに和ませるものがあった。秋月先生は古武士然として旧き良き日本を象徴・体現するような存在であったからである。

ハーンの授業時間は当初27時間で英語とラテン語を教えるというハードなものであったが一年後の新学期からは週20時間に負担軽減がなされている（1892年9月18日、西田千太郎への手紙より）。当時は50分授業で6時間目まであり、土曜日も4時間の授業体制を組んでいた。休み時間は10分で昼休みは50分であった。中島最吉氏が『熊本英学史』（昭和60年刊・本邦書籍）においてハーンの熊本時代を扱った論文「ラフカディオ・ハーン」の第二章、第三節「第五高等中学校におけるハーン」によれば、ハーンは土曜日には授業がなかった由、それゆえ当初普段の授業負担30時間のうち空き時間が3時間しかなく、かなり負担の大きなものであったことが窺える。その上出版のための原稿書きとその細微にわたる推敲である。熊本時代の明治24年（1891）11月19日に来日後最初の書物『知られぬ日本の面影』（Glimpses of Unfamiliar Japan）を上梓してからそれ以後亡くなる明治37年（1904）9月26日までほとんど毎年1冊のペースで本を書いていくという仕事ぶりであった。

松江時代のハーンは英語の授業では学生の書く英作文を訂正し、内容に関して適切なコメントの添え書きをしていた。平成16年（2004）6月に熊本県立図書館で見つかった大谷正信と田辺勝太郎の2人の生徒のハーンによる英作文添削のガラス乾板の判読、復元がアラン・ローゼン、西川盛雄共著による『ラフカディオ・ハーンの英作文教育』（平成23年刊、弦書房）として出版されたが、これによればハーンが生徒に与えていた課題は概して次のようなものであったことが分かっている。

◇生き物：「ホトトギス」「梟」「鳶」「鶯―（日本の歌鳥）―」「ホタル」「百足」「亀」「蛙」
◇植物（花）：「牡丹」「蓮」
◇スポーツ：「剣道」「相撲」「水泳」
◇神々と神社：「七福神」「松江の春日（神社）について」
◇民芸品：「漆器」
◇生活品：「米」「茶」
◇人事：「消防士」「最も偉大な日本人」
◇実用面：「書店に本を注文すること」「父へ」「ラフカディオ・ハーン先生へ」
◇趣向：「私の嫌いなもの」「世に最も怖ろしいものは何か」
◇祭日と行事：「雛祭り」「天皇誕生日」「先週土曜日の運動会」
◇霊的なもの：「幽霊」「創造者」「天皇」「祖先を敬う理由は何か？」
◇自然風景：「大山という山」「宍道湖」「宍道湖をボートで行く」
◇古代様式：「古代日本の様式：住居」「古代日本の様式：衣服」

これらを英語で作文するということは生徒たちにとっては英語力向上の契機となり、ハーンにとっては来日してすぐ、日本事情を理解するのに格好のものであったであろう。生徒たちには自らの生活経験に基づくものを書かせ、実用面では英語の手紙の書き方を教えるというハーン先生の授業は当時としては斬新なものであったであろう。いずれにしてもアメリカで長年新聞記者をしていたハーンには来日当初、松江という新たな場において日本を「取材して・書く」というジャーナリストとしてのスタンスが色濃く反映されていたことは間違いないであろう。

　しかし第五高等中学校では、松江時代とは違って学生たちはソフィストケイトされ、知的好奇心も高く多様になっていた。ハーンは熊本に来てからは作品「九州の学生とともに」の中にあるように英作文の授業では〈人が最も永く記憶にとどめるものは何か？〉〈文学における不滅なるものは何か？〉そして時にはアーサー王伝説を学生に聞かせて「東洋固有の考え方」にもとづいてこの伝説譚について意見を述べることを課題として出していた。

　ハーンの熊本時代の授業も松江時代同様自らの英語を直接聞かせて板書し、学生はその内容をノートに取り、理解し、その場で対応していくのである。この『熊本高校時代に於けるLafcadio Hearnの英語教授』（以後『講義ノート』と略称する）にみられるように授業はよく準備され、用いられている事例も身近で豊富なものであった。

　当時英語の授業は一般的に予め西洋のものをテキストとして定め、その内容に解説を加えるといった授業が多かった。ハーンもまた西洋の良き作品を授業で使っていた。たとえば他のクラスまたは学年ではThomas Carlyle（トマス・カーライル）を取り上げていたことは今日残されている試験問題を通して分かっている。また、シェークスピアの『ヴェニスの商人』やギリシャ神話の『ティトノスの物語』などを生徒に話して聞かせていたし、作品「九州の学生とともに」（"With Kyūshū Students"）で記されているようにギリシャ神話のエディポスとスフィンクスの話やSir Thomas Malory（サー・トマス・マロリー）の『アーサーの死』を話して聞かせていたことが分かっている。

　しかしハーンの視点は西洋優位の啓蒙的、宣教的なものではなかった。したがって西洋優位の視点が顕著だった前任者のエバー・クラミーに対する評価は厳しい。クラミーはイギリス文学のGeorge Eliot（ジョージ・エリオット＝本名・Mary Ann Evans）の作品をテキストとして使っていたが、エリオットの英文を直接読ませることはストーリーの学生に対する親近性に悖るだけでなく、難渋な英語に触れさせることになり、却って学生には少なからざる違和感を生じさせてしまうことになる、としている。ハーンはこの前任者の授業を批判して日本の中学生に「ジョージ・エリオットの『サイラス・マナー』や『ジョン・ハリファックス』のような長ったらしい重畳的重・複文の半哲学的文章」を読ませてどのような意味があるのだ、といった不満を述べている（1891年11月、チェンバレンへの書簡・追伸）。

かくしてハーンの英語授業はこの『講義ノート』を見る限り、前任者の方法とは異なり、英語そのものの用法や語源に焦点を当て、授業のスタンスにおいては軸足を西洋の側にではなく学ぶ日本人学生の側に置いている。学生たちの日常生活から遊離した抽象的で分かり難いテキストの作品世界を〈文字〉の読みを通して追っかけるのではなく、ネイティヴ・スピーカーではない日本人学生が外国語である英語を身に付けるには何が必要か、という根本的な視点に立っている。かくしてハーンは学生に英語で直接話しかけ、取り上げる事例は具体的で身近なものを用いながら、説明は英語そのものの規則性や語法や語源を理解することに心を砕いていた。例えば採られている素材は授業の舞台である熊本や九州に関する「阿蘇」「水前寺」「白川」「熊本」「大宰府」「筑後川」「霧島」などが出てくるだけでなく、人名では「秋月胤永」「西郷隆盛」の名が出てくるのは印象的である。そして学習者が語句の記憶をより確かなものとして定着させるために、語の語源的説明を駆使し、視覚的な図解による説明も取り込んでいる。これは大脳の効率的な記憶と学習したことの保持能力に関して言語習得には欠かせないことであった。

（2）ニューオーリンズ時代の論説記事

　実はこれには理由があった。ハーンはすでに来日前のニューオーリンズ時代に言語に関するいくつかの論説記事を『タイムズ・デモクラット』紙に書いている。すでに外国語の習得問題に熱心であったハーンはニューオーリンズでスペイン語に興味を持ち、すでに19世紀後半のフランス文学の英語への翻訳作業を続け、日常的なクレオールの混淆文化圏での生活の中で「言語」習得への関心は並々ならぬものがあったと考えられる。
　ハーンはニューオーリンズ時代の論説記事「言語学習における目と耳の効用」（"The Use of the Eye or the Ear in Learning Languages" 4/11/1885）で当時の言語学者ミシェル・ブレアルの講演内容を紹介する形で「話し言葉は音声による概念の原初的媒体であり、書き言葉はそうした概念を耐久性のある記号で定着する技術である」と述べ、耳からの言語教授の重要性を強調している。そして言語の自然の法則として音声言語は文字言語の基盤になることについて述べている。
　事実ハーンは、すでに述べたように、学生に身近な話題を用いて直接英語で解説し、問いかけ、反応を求めるという対話方式で進めていたことはこの考え方と符合する。また、ハーンの言語習得における実際面の観点からみて、「音」（耳）から「目」（文字）への方向性は確固としてあり「言葉を音声的に身につければその後、教育ある人が綴字法や文法、文法細則、さらにその言語で書かれた文学作品の美を学ぶのが非常にやさしくなる」と述べている。そしてハーンはルイジアナのクレオールの人々は2、3カ国語を特に学校で学ぶわけでもないのに自由に操れるようになるという話に触れ、音声を通した早い時期での訓練が大切であることを指摘する。

「外国語の問題」("A Language Question" 5/16/1885) において外国語を学ぶことの大切さについて触れている。まず、「テニソン、ブラウニング、ロングフェロー、ロセッティのような大詩人たちは外国語の知識なしにその偉業を成し遂げたのだろうか?」と問い、「外国語を知ることによって、自国語に対する知識は広まり、深くなる」ことを述べている。さらに、ものには歴史的背景があり、謂れがある。そこには進化論的な原理が関与しているとするのである。ここにはハーンの Herbert Spencer（ハーバート・スペンサー）からの影響が見て取れるが、言語もまた例外ではない。それは自ずから言語学習において語源を知ることの大切さにも通じるというわけである。事実ハーンの『講義ノート』では英語の語彙の謂れ（語源）の説明が頻出する。しかもその内容は身近で興味深い。例えば週の曜日の言い方にある北欧ゲルマンの神々の名前から来る神話的語源について解説する。またギリシャ語由来の climate（気候）、ラテン語由来の city（市）、ヴァイキングのデーン語由来の gale（強風）、サンスクリット語由来の storm（嵐）など、種々の語源的説明は学習者に「そうだったのか」と言わしめる。ハーンはこの論説において記憶の定着のストラトジーとして語源研究の大切さを提案しているのである。

ハーンはこの論説で「一つの言語に習熟するということはなかなか難しいことなのである。けれども語の歴史をたずねての語源研究は大いに役立つだろう。いったんその語の歴史を知ると、その語は記憶から去ることはけっしてない」と言う。ハーンはこのようにすでに来日する前から、学習者が語の謂れ（あるいは語源）を学ぶことの重要さを指摘していることは興味深い。事実ハーンの英語授業では語源的説明が多く活用されているが、そこには歴史や神話に由来する語源的知識の興味深さと重要さを少しでも学生に伝えようとするハーンのスタンスを読み取ることができるのである。

またハーンは論説記事「頭のなかの辞書」("Mental Dictionary" 11/16/1884) の中で言語習得、特に語や文法の獲得と記憶保持に関して大脳が大きな役割を果たすことをすでに指摘していた。大脳は言語の構成要素が〈記憶〉として保持されている「素晴らしい館」なのである。

言語は表現と理解においては意味の世界に関してメンタルな思考のプロセスの反映である。ある言語の語彙や一定の規則性を記憶し、定着させることによって言語能力は増す。この記憶を堅固なものにするためには語や慣用句の謂れ（語源）についての知識を持つことが望ましい。

後に「意味論」という領域をつくった言語学者として知られる Michel Breal（ミシェル・ブレアル）は言語は「物の概念そのものが精神に刻印される最初のものである。」とし、概念とそれを刻印する記号としての言語との関係に注目した。そして物の概念の把握に関連して「われわれは独特な能力を有している」という。この「独特な能力」とは言語形式による意味づけに関わる能力である。そしてこのブレアルは「言語学者は言語研究に進化論的方法を採用し、…われわれを知性的作業の作業現場の内側に案内する」というのである。

知性的作業の作業現場の内側とは人間の言葉による指示物への命名プロセスと表現と理解をめぐる推論のプロセスのことである。ハーンはこの論文の中で人間の言葉による指示物への命名プロセスの多義性（ポリセミー、polysemy）の例として「title（タイトル）」と「key（キー）」の2例を出している。前者では「著作物」「法律」「肩書き」「宗教」においては「タイトル」という語は異なった意味内容をもち、後者では「音楽上」「機械操作上」「著作物上」において「キー」という語はそれぞれ異なった意味内容をもつことを指摘する。必要に応じて展開される語の意味の拡張とその結果として生じてくる語の多義性は概念形成に関して人間の〈独特な能力〉の一側面であるに違いないのである。この『講義ノート』の中でも、ハーンはplayの例を出して「遊び」と「演劇」の同音（綴）異義（あるいは多義性）の事実とその使い方について例示する。またsoundやfastの多義性について学生に教えている。さらに同じpaperでも単・複で意味が異なることを説明する。このように形式としての語が指し示す内容との意味関係で、拡張という知性的作業を経て出来上がっていく語の意味の多様性については並々ならぬ注意を払っているのである。

（3）『講義ノート』の内容

それでは〈ラフカディオ・ハーンの英語教授〉の方法を証すこの『講義ノート』の内容とはどのようなものであったのか述べてみたい。まずは授業の初めに夏休みに経験したことについて英語で書くことをクラス全員の学生に求める。ものを書くに際して人は実際の経験に基づいて書くことがもっとも入りやすいことをハーンは知っていたのである。そして英語を書くに際して「間違いを恐れるな」「間違いを通して人は賢くなる」というのである。

学習者にとって難しいのは語の綴りや辞書的意味を覚えることではない。これらは辞書や参考書を丁寧に調べれば分かるものである。むしろ難しいのは母語使用者が無意識に使い分けている語やイディオムの微妙なニュアンス（shades）を理解することや語の背後にある謂れや語源を心得ることなのである。この『講義ノート』全体を通して似て非なる2つの語のニュアンスの違い（差異）や同じ語であっても冠詞の有無によって意味が使い分けられる場合や同じ語でも単数・複数で意味が異なる場合や語法上の前置詞の使い方のルール（一般規則）については特に詳しく述べているのも故なしとしないのである。

ハーンはまずcountryという語の「国」と「田舎」の使い分けを説明する。日本人学習者には気がつきにくい点であるが、後者にはtheが付く。これに対してyour countryのように人称代名詞の属格が付く場合は「いなか」ではなく「国」になるとハーンはいう。

さらにハーンは解説する。「木」にはtreeとwoodがありtreeは生きている「立木」であるがwoodは立木が切られた後の「材木」の意味となる。「テーブルは木で出来ている」の「木」は英語ではtree（立木）ではなくwood（材木）なのである。

動詞の場合はどうであろうか。ハーンはcongratulateとcelebrateの差異を問い、この違いを説明しようとする。どちらも「祝う、祝福する」の意味である。しかしその用法は大きく異なる。前者は人を祝うのに対して後者は事業の成果、または催し（イベント）などを祝うのである。I congratulate you. は「私はあなたとともに喜びます。（おめでとう）」という意味で聞き手と〈共に〉喜ぶことを示唆している。ハーンはここで接頭辞[con-]のはたらきに言及するのである。ちなみにWe celebrate his victory.（私は彼の勝利を祝福します）では祝福されるのは「彼」ではなく「彼の勝利」というひとつの成果なのである。

　実はこれは現代の言語能力（language faculty）に通じる考え方である。言語は語用論的には「伝達の手段」であるが、認知論的にはコミュニケーションの場における推論（思考）のプロセスの反映である。ここでは人を祝福する場合はcongratulate、事業の成果や催しの場合はcelebrateである。日本語で同じ「祝う、祝福する」の意味であっても両者の使い分けの差異が分かる識別力こそ言語能力に違いないのである。

　ハーンは日本人学生のよく間違う例として色の表し方があるという。同じ色であっても暗い（dark）と明るい（bright (light)）があり、あるいは暖色のwarmがあり、生気のない色のdeadがある。色合いにはshades（ニュアンス）やtints（色調）の違いがあり2色が混淆された場合の英語の言い方を詳細に説明し、語の後に来る語が強調された色として主要語となることを指摘する（greenish greyはグレイの一種なのである）。

　形容詞の場合はどうであろうか。「高い」はまずはhighとtallである。前者は例えば「山」に用いて後者は「人」に用いると説明する。そしてhighは社会的地位が高く重要かつ影響力のある人物といった意味に拡張されて用いるがtallはそのようなことはない。さらにhighの反意語はlowであるがtallの反意語はshortであって同じ「高い」と言ってもその内容が異なることを説明する。

　ハーンの特筆すべき着眼点は同じ様な意味でも丁寧表現（politeness）に触れて説明しているところである。言語学では「語用論」といわれる領域でとりわけ重要な分野である。たとえば、人の身体的特徴として「細い」という語にはthinがあり、その反対にはfatがある。これをそのまま人に用いると文法的に正しくても社会的には誤りとされる。ここには語用論的な規則が働くからである。一般的に「やせた」人に直接thinを、「太った」人にfatを用いたりはしない。失礼だからである。ここでは〈失礼な言い方を避ける〉という語用論的「規則」が働くのである。ハーンはここでthinではなくslender（すらりとした）を、fatではなくstout（がっしりした）を用いることを紹介する。話し手の言葉使いには聞く相手に対する評価的な心配りが反映されていなければならないからである。このようにハーンは話し手と聞き手の間にある言葉の心理的効果についてよく理解しており、既に120年前の英語の授業でこのことについて触れていたことは斬新で、特筆すべきことであると思われる。

気候を表す climate と天候を表す weather との比較において climate はギリシャ語の [klima] に由来すると言うとき、ハーンは中学生だから英語の授業でギリシャ語などに触れる必要はない、とはけっして思わなかった。むしろ語源に触れて授業の内容に厚みを持たせ、学生が語を記憶する上で語の謂れに興味をもつことの大切さを伝えている。強風を表す gale の由来はデンマーク語（Danish）の「気が狂う」を表す [gal] に由来すると授業で触れるとき、ハーンは、英語はその昔デーン人、したがってヴァイキングの古ノルド語からの影響を受けていることを念頭に置いていたに違いない。しかも聴講する学生たちのレベルへの信頼の証しとしてハーンは授業で嵐（storm）の由来は「ばら撒く、撒き散らす」を意味するサンスクリット語の [Stur] から来ていることを解説し、台風は古代ギリシャ神話の嵐の神タイフォン [Typhon] から来ていることを述べている。

　語の謂れといえばハーンは夏の「土用」の頃の暑さについて神話的説明の紹介を行う。たとえば Dog-days（土用）の語源の説明が興味深い。土用の頃には真昼に太陽と大犬座の首星であるシリウスが同時に天上に位置する。この頃には天上はますます明るく、地上はますます暑くなるという昔からの言い伝えを用いてその謂れを説明するのである。

　英語の週の曜日の説明に際してもハーンはゲルマンやローマの神話に由来することを説く。「日曜」と「月曜」は太陽と月に捧げられた日で古代北欧のチュートン民族は太陽や月を崇めていたことをまず紹介する。火曜は勇気を表す神（軍神）[Tyr]、水曜は神々の父（叡智の神）[Woden]、木曜はハンマーを持った力ある神（雷神）[Thor]、金曜は Woden の妻で美神 [Frigga] など北欧神話の神々の名に由来し、土曜はローマ神話の農耕の神 [Saturn] から来ていることを説く。それでなくても英語の初学者には覚え難い曜日の言い方である。このような説明を受ければ少なからず学生は英語に興味をもったに違いない。語はその謂れを知ることによって記憶がより定かになる。語は単なる機能的な記号で終始するものではない、寧ろ語にはそれなりの謂れや理由（歴史・物語）があるのである。

　ハーンはさらに似て非なるものを提起しながらさながら生物学の基礎のような授業を展開する。鳥は飛ぶ。蝙蝠も飛ぶ。蝙蝠の翼（飛膜）は皮膚の一部で毛で覆われている。しかし鳥の翼は羽で覆われている。鳥は卵を産むが蝙蝠は卵は産まない。その代わり雛をミルクで育てる。その意味で蝙蝠は哺乳類である、と解説していく。

　鳥の中には飛ぶものと飛べないものがある。ダチョウ（ostrich）は飛ばない代わりに走るのが速い。昔ニュージーランドに大きさが5〜6メートルもあるモア（moa）という鳥がいたが絶滅してしまった。生命体は種として生き残るためには周囲の自然環境への適応が必須である。適応するためには個体のある種の能力が特化・進化する。その結果として身体的特徴も変化する。ハーンの授業の中にはこのように進化論を髣髴とさせる内容が組み込まれている。そういえばハーンはすでにニューオーリンズ時代にハーバート・スペンサーの『第一原理』を読み、おのずから進化論に共鳴していたことが思い出される。

　ハーンはすでに日本語的な発想にもとづく英語語句の理解ならぬ誤解の危うさを指摘す

る。ハーンの指摘は日本人学習者の盲点を突く。会話では your body, his body とは普通言わない。英語で body と言うとき、それは「死体」(corpse) を意味する。"I am sick."（私は気分がすぐれない）の意味で "My body is sick." とは言わない。対照的に日本語では「私の体」「君の体」「彼の体」といった言い方はごく普通の言い方である。

さらに『講義ノート』においては、ハーンの英語授業の特徴は図解を用いるということである。日本語で「足」といっても英語では foot, leg, thigh と3種類あり、ハーンはそれぞれの部位を説明するのに「足」の図を用いている。靴が履けるのは foot だけだという説明は興味深い。同様に日本語でいう「手」も hand, forearm, upper arm と分けて図解している。手の指は日本語では5本であるが、英語では thumb（親指）だけは別に考えられているがハーンの説明はそれぞれの指の呼び方を図解して説明する。また身近なもので「帽子」には英語で hat と cap があるが、hat は縁のある帽子、cap はつばがないか前にだけある帽子である。ハーンはこれを図に描いて分かりやすく説明する。

生活に根ざした動作における比較文化の例としてハーンは「のこぎり」のひき方に言及する。日本人の大工はのこぎりを自分の方に向けて引くが西洋の大工はのこぎりを体から向こうの方に離す方向で押すのである。また何かものを書くとき、西洋人はペンを使うときは手首（wrist）を使うが、日本人は肘（elbow）を使うことをハーンは指摘する。ペンマンシップの文化と毛筆文化の相違である。このようにハーンの授業はどこまでも具体的で日常的な生活の営みの中に東西文化の差異を指摘している点、興味深いものがある。

「都市」(city) と「町」(town) と「村」(village) の区別は現代の英語学習者にも気になるところである。ハーンはまず city は当時の感覚で 50,000 人以上の人が住んでいる所といい、town よりはるかに大きいところだという。熊本での授業ということもあってか例として東京、京都、大阪に次いで熊本を例として上げている。続いて大宰府はどうか、と問いかけて、大宰府は大きくはあるが village だと言っている。ハーンによれば village は大きな農業市場であって物の生産・製造（産業）の場がないところと説明する。さらに town と village の区別については一般的に前者では city とならんで物の製造が行われているが後者では農業従事者が多くいる所と説明する。さらに town ではあるが物の製造をしていない場所として港町を指摘している。ここで興味深いことは、同じ港でも port の由来はラテン語であり、harbor はスカンジナヴィア由来の言語であることを述べ、ここでも語源的説明を行っていることである。さらに興味深いことに、英語史的に city はラテン語の [civitas] から来ているいわば英語の外来語であり、town はアングロ・サクソン系の古英語から来ているいわば本来の英語であることについて触れている。これはレベルは高く、英語教授上の視点がしっかりと抑えられており、しかもこれは学生に英語の興味を持たせるためのすぐれた英語教授法になっている。次の例はどうであろうか。

"When was Kumamoto Castle besieged?"（いつ熊本城は包囲されたのですか？）

"In the 10th year of Meiji."（明治 10 年です）

この例は二つの意味で興味深い。一つは文法的に前置詞の語法（usage）の具体例として一定のまとまった期間を表す用法としての in の説明である。もう一つはハーンは熊本を舞台とした歴史的な大事件を教室の話題にしていることである。この例文は西南戦争で熊本城が薩軍に包囲され、攻められた時のことを念頭においているが、このような例を示すことによって熊本という町と英語への関心が増し加わると考えられる。実際のハーン作品でも「橋の上」「願望成就」は西南戦争のことが背景知識として配されている。他にも "go" と副詞的小辞との結合の例を説明するに当たって "The River Shirakawa flows BY." という例を出して熊本市内を流れる「白川」を取り上げて "by" の説明を行っている。

　日本人学習者のよく戸惑う例として英語には定冠詞（the）がある。他方日本語には冠詞はない。ハーンはこのことを踏まえて英語の授業では冠詞の説明を怠らない。人の固有名詞の前はもちろん、固有名詞の特徴をもった山や川の呼称の前にも *the Mt. Aso のように the を用いてはならぬことを説く。ただし the mountain of Aso のように前置詞 of を用いた句の前には the が来なければならないことを対比的に説明している。

　言語には意味の拡張として比喩表現がある。隠喩、換喩、擬人法などあるものを別のものに喩（たと）えて言うのである。「なぞり」「みたて」といわれる意味の世界がこれに当たる。ハーンは『講義ノート』の中で「風の音」の多種多様な特徴を多様な「人の声」にみたてて擬人法を駆使した活き活きとした英語表現を紹介する。〈風が吹く〉様を、「口笛をヒューッと吹くように（whistle）」「むせび泣くように（wail）」「呻くように（moan）」「ひそひそと囁くように（whisper）」「悲鳴を上げるように（shriek）」音をたてるといった具合である。比喩表現は拡張された新たな意味の創造である。学生は比喩表現に触れることによって豊かな言語の世界を実感することができる。ハーンの授業にはこの英語による比喩表現の妙味が配されていることは忘れられてはならない。

　さらに、ハーンは授業で語形成において小さくても大きな力をもつ指小辞の説明を行っていることは記憶されていていい。たとえば hamlet は村落を表すデーン語の [ham] に指小辞の [-let] が付いたものである。この [-let] を取り上げて英語における接尾辞付与による語の派生（拡張）の方法を例示している。指小辞は〈小ささ〉に加えて〈可愛さ〉〈親愛性〉を含意した概念を表わすが、英語にはこの種の語彙拡充の例は多い。『講義ノート』では他に book から booklet が出来ている例を示している。

　ハーンは『講義ノート』の中で前置詞の説明の方法にも心を砕いている。例えば into, across, through といった前置詞を説明するのにそれぞれの一般的ルール（general rule）を述べ、その基本概念を図解している。この方法は非常に明快で分かりやすく、有益かつ親切である。英語の前置詞に関しては辞書をみて理解しようとするが、at, in, on など基本的な前置詞の本質理解は日本人には難しい。ハーンはこれを図を示すことによって説明するのである。これは現代にも通じるイメージ・スキーマによる説明方式で当時としては

すこぶる斬新なものであったに違いない。

　以上ハーンが『講義ノート』で解説しているところを概略まとめてみたが、英語語法（English usage）の観点からはすぐれて充実した内容となっている。そしてこれは今から約120年前のハーンによる英語の授業なのである。

　　　（4）意義

　次にこの『講義ノート』の意義について述べてみたい。
　第1に、ハーンのお雇い外国人英語教師としての学生に対するスタンスに関してである。明治維新以降、お雇い外国人の日本の近代化に果した役割は大きかったがそれは概して文化・文明の西洋優位、東洋劣位の視点で西洋人教師による啓蒙的、宣教的なスタンスで授業が成されていたものが多かった。これはいわば上から下への目線で教え導くという教導型の授業であった。明治新政府も「脱亜入欧」の視点に立って「進んだ」西洋の文化・文明を導入することに余念がなかった。時代は富国強兵、殖産興業を合言葉に急速な近代化、西洋化に邁進していたのである。したがって高等教育の語学授業においては概ね西洋に軸足をシフトし、西洋の作家や思想家が書いたものをテキストとしていた。その結果として内容は日本人の生活実感から離れたものになる傾向が多かったのである。
　しかしハーンのスタンスはこれとは異なっていた。彼は松江時代と同様に学生には同じ目線で接し、教導型ではなく、人格的には等しく〈共に〉学ぶという共感型あるいは対話型の教師であった。事実ハーンは日本を理解・探求すべく日本人の生活ぶりや民俗学的な遺産や行事や自然風景などを直接知るという姿勢を一貫してもっていたのである。また授業に際しては日本古来の価値観に敬意を払い、秋月胤永のようにこれを体現している人に敬愛の情を持っていた。そして学生に対する授業のスタンスは学生たちのヴァナキュラー（土着的）な風土や文化を尊重し、実生活と結びついた実用的、実践的なものを授業に取り上げていた。これはこれまでにないお雇い外国人教師のあり方であった。
　第2にこの『講義ノート』には英語教師としてのハーンの確固たる近代的な英語学的手法が反映されている。それは授業では学生は「英語」そのものの語法（usage）や規則性について正しい知識を得る、というスタンスである。これは当り前のようであるが、当時にあって周囲は英語を通して西欧の文化・文明を〈学ぶ〉という雰囲気であった。しかしハーンはこれとは違い、言語（英語）の音声面の重視を前提にして正確な英語の知識を身につけるという現実的な視点を重視するものであった。言い換えればハーンの言語（英語）教育の目的は学習者の大脳の中に記憶されるべき「頭のなかの辞書」（Mental Dictionary）の充実を図るものであった。
　コミュニケーションの場においては言語の規則性についての知識がしっかり大脳内に定着していなければ妥当な語や文を産み出せず、また十分にこれを理解することができない。

このような観点からハーンは英語の規則性についての説明を念入りに行っている。その知識は大脳の中に蓄えられる。例えば will と shall の事例に基づく実践的な使い分けの規則性、定冠詞 the の使用規則、時間概念や空間概念に用いる基本的な前置詞の使用規則、名詞の単数・複数による意味の違い、さらに語法上の２つの似て非なる語の差異の説明などである。

言語能力とは、ある言語について妥当な表現と妥当でない表現とを自らチェックすることのできる能力である。たとえ誤った表現を産出した場合でもこれを即座に点検して修正することのできる能力である。これが可能になるためには正確な英語語法上の規則性についての知識が定着していることが前提である。ハーンは五高教師時代にすでにこのことを弁えて学生にしっかりとした英語の規則性についての知識が身に付くような工夫を凝らしていたのではないだろうか。このようにハーンはすでに明治27年（1894）の時点で授業を受ける学習者の心理に配慮しながら、英語教授法的に的を射た授業を行っていたことは驚きで、このことはもっと世に知られていいと思われる。

第３にハーンは授業に際しては身近なものを素材とし、学生には親しみをもって授業に参加できるように工夫していたことが窺える。この『講義ノート』に出てくる素材は「熊本城」、「水前寺」、「阿蘇」、「白川」「大宰府」など身近な熊本周辺の実名を用いて例文を作成している。他に五高キャンパス内の武道館であった「瑞邦館」の名も出てくる。この瑞邦館に掛かっていた秋月胤永先生の肖像画（油絵）の話も授業の素材として取り上げられている。また歴史上の人物としては西南戦争時に熊本城を包囲した「西郷隆盛」の名前も出てくる。興味深いことに日付の書き方の日英比較をするところで、想像上（imaginary）の住所（address）を書くところで例として「坪井」を用いている。これは当時ハーン自身が住んでいた第２旧居の住所（熊本市坪井西堀端町35）を使ったものであった。このように〈教材は身近で分かりやすいものを使用する〉というスタンスにおいて学生に英語に親しみ、興味をもたせるという工夫を凝らしていたことは特筆しておいていい。

前任のお雇い外国人教師の授業のテキストは George Eliot など古典的な英文学の原典であった。しかしハーンはこの考えは取らず、素材を日本人の生活にとって身近なものにし、実際の英語の語法的側面に焦点を当て、豊富な用例や図解（イメージ・スキーマ）による説明を加えることによって学生の英語への関心を身近なものにしようとしていた。この方策は学習者が英語に興味をもち、言語（英語）習得の上でも現実的・実用的な教授法に連なるものであった。実際この『講義ノート』を見ていくにつけても最近の斬新な文法書を見る思いである。

第４にこの『講義ノート』を通してハーンの英語の授業は共感型、対話型のスタイルをとっていたことが窺える。「～とは何か？」「～と～の違いは何か」「～と～との類似点は何か？」「～は～である。何故か？」といった問いかけが頻出する。学生にまず身近な問題を問いかけて注意を喚起し、次にその応えを模索させ、さらに説明を加えるというスト

ラテジーである。したがってこの『講義ノート』には基本的に「何か？」（what）、「何故か？」（why）と問いかける場面が多い。ここにはハーンの対話による授業の進め方のストラテジーが反映されている。言語（英語）には文や語を形成するルール（規則性）が存在するが社会的な約束事としての語用論的なものもある。ハーンはこの両者に目配りしながら身近で具体的な事例の提示とその解説を忘れない。これはハーンの優れた英語教師としての見識を証明しているといえよう。

さらにこの『講義ノート』を見る限り、ハーンの講義は簡潔な会話口調で進んでいく。冒頭「各自、順番に夏休みのことを話してください。―なにか不思議な、面白い体験をしたり、楽しかったり、美しいものを見たりしたことをです。」から始まるこのセリフは『講義ノート』とは言え、教壇上の教師の息遣いまで伝わってくるようである。「countryという語は難しいですよ。皆さんが "I came back to my country." と言ったとしましょう。英語でその意味は…」と続いて "country" の二つの意味説明とその使い分けの基準について説明する。また講義の運びはクエスチョン・アンド・アンサーの対話型が多い。例えばハーンは「空の青は世界中同じですか？」と問うて「いいえ、空の青は天頂では濃く、地（水）平線に行くにつれて薄くなります」と説明したりするのである。

"Give an example. …"（例を出して下さい），"Remember …"（忘れないで下さい）などと文法上の命令文で始まる文を用いることによって学生との心理的距離を縮め、調節している。"Yes", や "No" の会話口調や "Did you feel the earthquake the other day?"（先日、地震の揺れを感じましたか？）などの問いかけがよく用いられている。このようにハーンの授業は一方的な講話ではなく、学生の授業に参画する余地を恒に保証してくれていることが特徴としてある。

第5にこの『講義ノート』によって松江時代と熊本時代の英語教師ハーンの比較研究が可能になるという点である。松江時代は学生に英作文の添削を行っていた。学生に与えた課題はいかにも日本的なものであった。ここではハーンは英語教師としての英文訂正とコメントの付記が重要な作業であった。

当初ハーンは何よりも来日してまだ日が浅く、エキゾティズムと相俟って日本のことを知りたいと思う心には大きなものがあった。そしてジャーナリストとして日本のことを取材して書き、これを西洋に紹介することがハーンの来日当初からの関心事であった。学生による英作文の添削は学生には英語の練習・訓練であったが、ハーンにとっては「日本」を手っ取り早く知る（取材）する格好の方策であったのである。

今回の熊本時代の『講義ノート』については対象となる学生は松江時代の学生たちよりも年齢も上であった。松江時代に比して学生たちは知的にものごとを一般化したり抽象化したりする能力に優れ、言語（英語）の一般的な規則性を理解するのに十分な知的発達を遂げていた。彼らは事例に基づいてある規則性を理解するという科学的思考も可能な年齢になっていたのである。かくして熊本時代のハーンは松江時代のように来日したばかりの

スタンスは影を潜め、高等中学校の教壇に立つ教師として学生の合理的・体系的思考を鍛えるというスタンスが顕著になってきたのではないかと思われる。

　第6に語の謂れの説明に関って民話、説話などが活かされていることはハーンの授業に特徴的なことである。たとえば英語における曜日の名称の謂れがゲルマンの北欧神話とローマの神話に登場する神々に由来することの説明は実用英語的な発想にはない学習者の英語への知的関心を喚起する。

　民話からはハーン作品「夏の日の夢」にも出てくる〈若返りの泉〉の話がここでも使われている。これは語法の問題として冠詞（a, the）の使用を学ぶところである。最初"an"で出てくる"old man"が次に出てくるときは"the"を伴うが、英語の冠詞の使われ方の実例を親しみ易く庶民の古来の教訓を含んだ民話を活用して学んでいくことはいかにも味わいのある方法である。

　寓話もハーンは授業に活用する。ある農夫がお気に入りのキツネとガチョウと1袋の米を持って川を渡ろうとしている。渡しの舟はごく小さなもので1艘しかない。一度に一つずつしか向う岸に運べないのである。先にキツネを運び次にガチョウを運べばキツネはガチョウを食べてしまう。先にガチョウを運び次に米を運べばガチョウは米を食べてしまう。さてどうしたものか？という謎解きのような寓話である。答えはまずガチョウを運び、次にキツネを運ぶがその時帰りにガチョウを連れ戻す。次に米を運び、戻ってきて最後にガチョウを再び向う岸に運ぶとよい、ということになる。これは生徒たちにとって一寸した知的ゲームかもしれない。しかし英語の寓話に触れて謎解きを行うことは楽しい授業であったに違いない。

　最後に印象的であるのは高田力教授の序文の最後の謝辞に挙げられている方の名前である。一人は本来ならこの『講義ノート』の出版を引き受けてくれることになっていた北星堂主の中土義敬氏である。そしてもう一人は旧制富山高校で高田教授に恐らくはアドバイスを与えたであろう元同僚の木俣修氏である。木俣修は著名な歌人としてその名が今日に残っているが、ここにその名の記されてあることはひとつの喜びである。

（にしかわ・もりお　熊本大学客員／名誉教授）

出版にあたって

　このたび『熊本高校時代に於ける Lafcadio Hearn の英語教授』（以下『講義ノート』）が出版されることになり、嬉しくてなりません。今振り返るとこの歴史的な出版に立ち会う幸運は、私たち二人にはビギナーズ・ラックというしかありません。

　出版に至る経緯は、平川祐弘先生の「まえがき」の記載にあるとおりです。そこで、ここでは、『講義ノート』の発見から平川先生に届くまでの経緯を書き、読者の便宜に供したいと思います。

　平成19年春、北星堂の二代目社長故中土順平氏の出版関係の多数の遺品が、富山大学に移送されました。遺品には、ハーン関係の諸資料、戦前の高等教育用の英文教科書多数、あるいは日本の小説の英文訳書等がありました。中土家の縁につらなる千田は、移送の仲にたったいきさつからこれら遺品を整理するうちに、同年夏、今回の手書きの『講義ノート』を見つけました。

　しかし、千田はハーンの学術研究とは無縁であり、内容は英文であり、また、ハーンは有名な歴史上の人物で事績は調べ尽くされているものだと思い、『講義ノート』の内容はすでに出版され公表されているのだろうと、気にかけていませんでした。

　とはいえ、なんとなく気がかりで、仕事の合間にハーンの全集などで調べてみましたが該当する書籍がなさそうなのです。妙に胸が騒ぎ、千田は旧知のマリ・クリスティーヌに『講義ノート』を見せました。

　マリ・クリスティーヌは、この『講義ノート』をみて驚き興奮したことを今も忘れることができません。授業でのハーンは身近な題材を用い、誰にでも分かりやすく、リズミカルな美しい英語を教え、学生たちもこれに応えて熱心にノートを取って学んでいたことが手に取るようにわかりました。日本の文化を愛し、その素晴らしさを外国に伝えることができるように英語を学んで欲しいというハーンの思いが伝わってきます。また、どんな人にも上下などはなく人と人とは対等であるということを、一所懸命に伝えていたことが良くわかります。100年以上も前の講義なのに今も新鮮です。マリ・クリスティーヌは、富山大学で、異文化交流の観点からハーンと現在の自分自身の立場を比較しながら『講義ノート』の研究をはじめました。

　そうこうするうちに、マリ・クリスティーヌは知人の紹介で平川先生とお会いする機会に恵まれ、千田ともどもお会いし、『講義ノート』を先生に鑑定していただきました。

　それ以後、平川先生は「これは、早く出版すべきものだ」とおっしゃって、強力なエンジンとなって、内容の吟味から何からなにまで、出版の初めから終わりまで引っ張ってくださいました。この『講義ノート』が既に研究者の間で話題になっているとわかり、私た

ちは、今さらながら今回の出版の意義や重大さを、思い知りました。

　途中平川先生はどんなにか私たちを歯がゆくお思いになっていただろうと推測できるだけに、私たちを幸運の渦の中に一緒に入れてくださったご恩に、感謝の言葉もありません。

　最後になりますが、私たちに幸運を授けてくださりお世話になった方々に、心からお礼を申し上げます。遺品を快くご提供くださった中土家の皆様、膨大な資料の搬送にご尽力くださった若林久嗣様ありがとうございました。平川祐弘先生、西川盛雄先生ありがとうございました。富山大学前学長西頭德三様、富山大学学長遠藤俊郎様、富山八雲会前会長南日康夫様、木村嵯峨子様、友枝觀水様、尾座本雅光様、栗林裕子様、松井玖美様、ありがとうございました。

　　　　　千田篤　（富山八雲会会員）
　　　　　マリ・クリスティーヌ　（異文化コミュニケーター、富山大学客員特別研究員）

「ノート」の原作者＝友枝高彦（明治31年11月、東京帝国大学の頃、友枝觀水氏蔵）

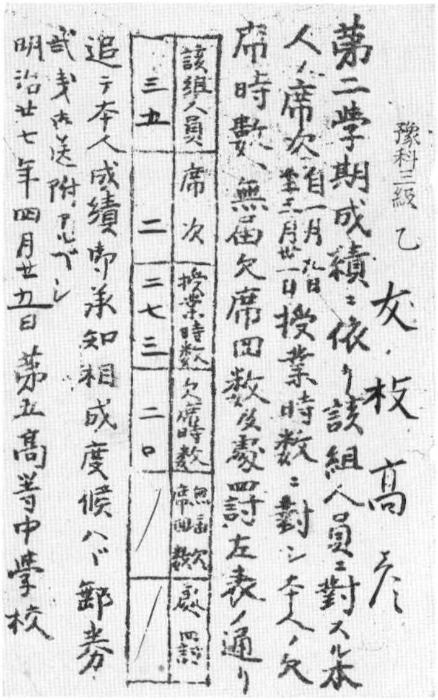

〈中・右〉
友枝高彦が第五高等中学校予科3級に在学中の成績表（明治27年4月25日、家族にあてて送られている、友枝觀水氏蔵）

友枝「ノート」を筆写した高田力（昭和5年、富山高等学校教授の頃、『富高一代記』から、富山大学附属図書館蔵）

中土義敬（昭和2年、北星堂のLafcadio Hearn Series 刊行案内パンフレットから、富山大学附属図書館蔵）、高田力が筆写した友枝「ノート」をさらに筆写し保管した

あとがき

　この度『ラフカディオ・ハーンの英語教育』が発刊される運びとなりました。本書は、ハーン研究の第一人者である平川祐弘氏、西川盛雄氏、ノートの発見者である千田篤氏、マリ・クリスティーヌ氏、そして発刊のためにご支援を頂いた松井玖美氏、弦書房小野静男氏など、ハーンを愛する多くの方々の熱意と努力が結実した１冊であります。書としての根幹は、編者である友枝高彦氏、高田力氏、中土義敬氏が関わられたノートおよびそのコピーではありますが、平川先生と西川先生のご説明を頂いたことにより，ハーンの教育者そして人間としての思いも伝わってくる、素晴らしい一冊となっています。ヘルン文庫を持つ富山大学を代表して、本書が発刊されることは大きな喜びであり、出版にご尽力された関係各位に対し心より感謝を申し上げます。特に指導的立場で、本書の発刊を牽引、実現してくださった平川先生には、重ねて深甚なる謝意を表させていただきます。

　現在大きく変化する社会・世界情勢の中で、事あるごとに「グローバル化への対応」が課題として語られています。科学技術、情報技術の急速な進歩・普及は、確かに世界の経済社会体制を大きく変え、今後もその流れは変わらぬことでありましょう。一方で、人々があまりにも時代の変化に翻弄され、人間として、あるいは国として、個が育んできた文化や伝統を軽視しがちなことに強く危惧も生じています。グローバル化する世界で大切なことは、混じり合う異なる文化の理解と共有であり、特に言語はその本質的役割を担っていると考えます。その意味で、ハーンが日本で行ってきた英語教育や文化活動、そして彼の生き様には、強く心をうたれるものがあります。ハーンは、今の時代にこそ求められる、人の心そして文化を継承することの大切さを伝えています。本書はまさにそのメッセージであり、ハーンを愛し、ハーンの思いを共有する関係者の皆さんの思いが詰まっています。

　富山大学では、ヘルン文庫を貴重な歴史的文化資産として、皆様の研究や文化活動に役立てていただけるよう，今後とも大切に保存保管に勤めて参ります。また人文学部、図書館の教職員を中心に、ハーン研究のさらなる発展を目指して参ります。皆様からも、引き続きご指導ご支援頂けますようお願い致します。

　　　　　　　　　　　　　　　　　　　　　2013年1月　富山大学長　遠藤俊郎

〈編著者略歴〉

平川祐弘（ひらかわ・すけひろ）

　1931年東京に生まれる。1953年東京大学教養学部教養学科卒業。仏伊給費留学生。1964年東大大学院比較文学比較文化課程担当助手。1992年東大定年退官、名誉教授。
著書、『和魂洋才の系譜』（1971, 現在は平凡社、博士論文）、『小泉八雲──西洋脱出の夢』（1981, サントリー学芸賞）『破られた友情──ハーンとチェンバレンの日本理解』（1987）『小泉八雲とカミガミの世界』（1988）『オリエンタルな夢──小泉八雲と霊の世界』（1996）『ラフカディオ・ハーン──植民地化・キリスト教化・文明開化』（2004, ミネルヴァ書房、和辻賞）、編著 Rediscovering Lafcadio Hearn（Global Oriental, 1997）, Lafcadio Hearn in International Perspectives（Global Oriental, 2006）, A la recherche de l'identité japonaise—le shintō interprété par les écrivains européens（L'Harmattan, 2012）『小泉八雲事典』（2000）『講座小泉八雲』（2009, 新曜社）。編訳『小泉八雲名作選集』六巻（講談社学術文庫）。

ラフカディオ・ハーンの英語教育
Lafcadio Hearn's English Lessons
──友枝高彦・高田力・中土義敬のノートから

2013年3月31日第1刷発行
2014年12月30日第3刷発行
監　修　富山大学附属図書館ヘルン文庫Ⓒ
　　　　平川祐弘Ⓒ
発行者　小野静男
発行所　弦書房
　　　　〒810-0041　福岡市中央区大名2-2-43ELKビル301
　　　　TEL 092-726-9885　FAX 092-726-9886
　　　　E-mail:books@genshobo.com
　　　　http://genshobo.com/
印　刷　アロー印刷株式会社
製　本　株式会社渋谷文泉閣

Ⓒ 2013
落丁・乱丁本はお取替えいたします
ISBN978-4-86329-085-3 C0021